JAMIE SMART'S

BUNNY VS MONKEY

THE GREAT BIG GLITCH!

David Fickling Books

THE PHOENIX

Adaptation, additional artwork and colours by Sammy Borras.
Cover design by Paul Duffield.
Cover illustration by Jamie Smart.

Bunny vs Monkey: The Great Big Glitch is a
DAVID FICKLING BOOK

Book 10 in the Bunny vs Monkey series, available from thephoenixcomic.shop and all good bookstores.

First published in
Great Britain in 2024 by
David Fickling Books
31 Beaumont Street
Oxford, OX1 2NP

978-1-78845-308-0 (Standard Edition)
978-1-78845-344-8 (Waterstones Exclusive Edition)
1 3 5 7 9 10 8 6 4 2

DAVID FICKLING BOOKS Reg. No. 8340307
A CIP catalogue record for this book is available from the British Library.
Printed and bound in China by Toppan Leefung.

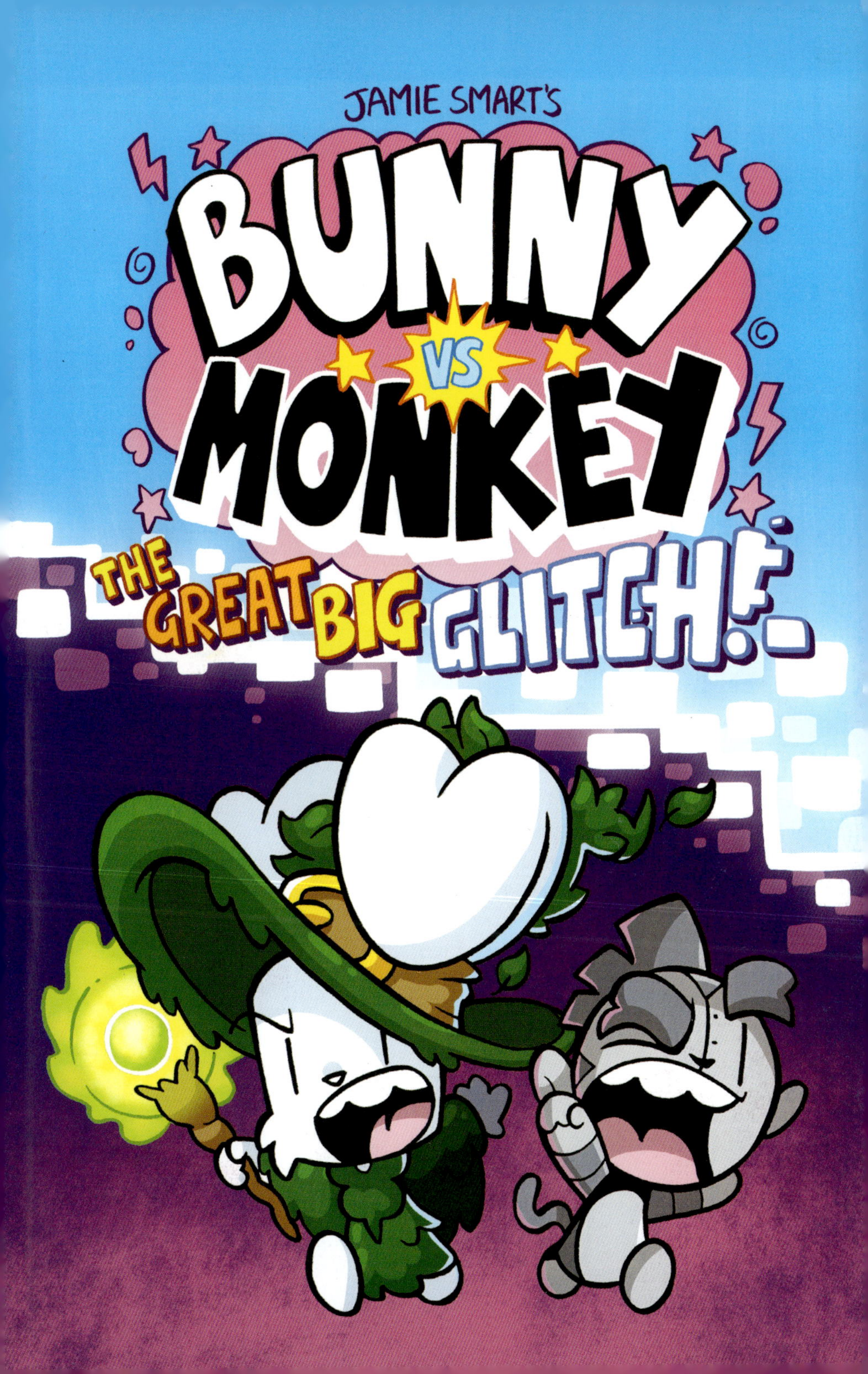
JAMIE SMART'S
BUNNY VS MONKEY
THE GREAT BIG GLITCH!

"MISTER BUM BUM"
BUNNY! WAKE UP!
I'M...NOT ASLEEP.
WAKE UPPPPP!
THIS IS AN EMERGENCY!!
WHATEVER IS THE MATTER, PIG?
I FOUND A LADYBIRD IN THE SNOW!
I NAMED HER MISTER BUM BUM.
BUT I THINK SHE GOT TOO COLD!
SHE'S NOT MOVING ANY MORE!

WELL, PIG, SOME CREATURES JUST DON'T LIKE THE WINTER VERY MUCH.
HELP HER! PLEEEEASE!
MAYBE... MAYBE IF WE PLACE HER DOWN CAREFULLY...
AND WISH REALLY REALLY HARD...
...A LITTLE BIT OF SUMMER MIGHT COME BACK!
AND THE LADYBIRD CAN FEEL WELL AGAIN!
THAT WAS AMAZING!
HMPH.
YOU HAVE IT, DON'T YOU?
GAH! LE FOX!
H...HAVE WHAT?

ZE GIFT! ZE SPECIAL POWER! ZE COMMAND OVER NATURE!!
OHHHH. WELL, YES, I THINK SO.
IT'S STRANGE, JUST RECENTLY I'VE BEEN ABLE TO COMMUNICATE WITH THE WOODS!
DING!
I CAN MAKE THINGS GROW JUST BY WILLING THEM TO BE.
PLINK!
PLUNK!
PLUNK!
HMPH.
AS SOMEONE WHO HAS BEEN AT ONE WITH ZE WOODS, I WOULD WARN YOU OF ZIS...
ZE ABILITY YOU HAVE IS IMMENSELY POWERFUL...
AND IT MUST ONLY BE USED WHEN YOU ARE IN GREAT DANGER!!

NYAH HA HA!
I FOUND ONE OF SKUNKY'S OLD INVENTIONS BEHIND THE TOILET!
BEWARE THE
SQUID BALL!
OH, YOU HAVE PICKED THE WRONG BUNNY TO...
!
NO, BUNNY! WHAT DID I JUST SAY?
BUT... BUT... SQUID BALL!
FIND... ANOTHER... WAY...
WELL, I DON'T THINK HITTING IT WITH A BRANCH IS GOING TO HELP US MUCH!
PAF!! PAF!!
HOI!!
YOU NEARLY STOOD ON MISTER BUM BUM!
MAY I?
OF COURSE!
YOU SEE, BUNNY? THERE IS ALWAYS ANOTHER SOLUTION.
PIG WITH A STICK?
PIG WITH A STICK.
WHACK! WHACK! WHACK! WHAC

WIENERS!
IT DOESN'T WORK! IT DOESN'T WORK!!
BLOP!
HOI!
YOU DEAL WITH IT!

SKUNKY! THE WIENER-COPTER 5000 WAS A DISASTER! IT BURST INTO FLAMES AND A HUNDRED HOT DOGS FELL OUT!!
YOU'RE RIGHT! IT NEEDS MORE HOT DOGS!
NO, IT NEEDS SCRAPPING! I COULD HAVE BEEN REALLY HURT!
WELL THEN, MAYBE YOU SHOULDN'T HAVE TAKEN IT WITHOUT ASKING!
IT LOOKED FUN! WHAT WAS I SUPPOSED TO DO?
HANG ON, WHO WAS THAT BEAVER WHO USED TO TEST DRIVE YOUR INVENTIONS?
ACTION BEAVER?
STAN, WAS IT?
ACTION BEAVER.
SUSAN.
ACTION BEAVER! THAT'S IT! GIVE HIM A CALL, FAR BETTER HE RISKS HIS LIFE IN THESE THINGS BEFORE I INEVITABLY STEAL THEM!
EMERGENCY ACTION BEAVER HOTLINE
BRING BRING!

FSNCK!
MALLO?
ACTION BEAVER! YOU'RE NOT ANSWERING YOUR PHONE!
WE NEED YOU!!
...TO TEST DRIVE MY NEW INVENTION, THE WIENER ROCKET 5000!!

OH MAN, THIS LOOKS FUN! WHICH BUTTON MAKES IT GO FWOOSH?!!
BOOP! BEEP! BOOP! BOOP!
NO, MONKEY! THAT'S NOT FOR YOU! NOT FOR...
FWOOSH!
...YOOOOOUU.
FLMPP!
AUGH!
I COULD HAVE SERIOUSLY INJURED MYSELF!

"SHARK ATTACK"
A PICTURESQUE BEAUTY SPOT IN THE WOODS...
A YOUNG COUPLE ENJOYING A PICNIC...
...BUT WHAT MENACE SPEEDS TOWARDS THEM FROM THE DEEP?!

NYAH HA HA! SURPRISE, LOSERS!!
YOU'RE ABOUT TO GET CHOMPED BY THE
SHARK CANNON!
SHRIEK! RUN AWAY!
WAIT! I HAVEN'T WORKED OUT HOW TO TURN THE SAFETY CATCH OFF YET!
MEH! I'LL JUST CHASE YOU THROUGH THE WOODS WITH IT!
CHOMP CHOMP CHOM
PLAP! PLAP!

MEH HEH!
CHOMP CHOMP!
HEH HEH HEH!
PLAP! PLAP!
HEH...
OOF!
TRIP!
CHOOM!
RRGH! NOW MY SHARK'S STUCK UP A TREE!!
AHEM! I THOUGHT THIS MIGHT HAPPEN, SO I BROUGHT YOU SOME EXTRA AMMO!
SKUNKY, YOU'RE A GENIUS!!

RELOAD, AND USE THIS SHARK TO KNOCK THE OTHER ONE DOWN!
HMM. NAH.
PLAP! PLAP!
SOMEONE ELSE CAN DEAL WITH THAT ONE!
OOF! NOT AGAIN!!
TRIP!
CHOOOM!!

CAN I HAVE ANOTHER SHARK, PLEASE?
HALF AN HOUR LATER...
JUST ONE MORE! PLEEEEASE!
OH, THIS IS A MUCH NICER SPOT FOR A PICNIC.

"DOCTOR PIG"
"DOCTOR PIG"
WILL SEE YOU NOW!
The Doctor is IN
DOCTOR PIG, I BURNT MY FOCACCIA AND NOW I FEEL SAD.
PUT MUD ON YOUR HEAD!

M... MUD?
ON YOUR HEAD!
NEXT!
DOCTOR PIG, I RAN TOO FAST AND FELL OVER A TREE!
MUD ON YOUR HEAD!
DOCTOR PIG -HIC- I CAN'T STOP -HIC- HICCUPPING!!
MUD. HEAD. MUD ON YOUR HEAD!

DOCTOR PIG! I TIED A ROCKET TO MY BACK BUT NOW I CAN'T REACH TO TURN IT OFF!
FOOOOOOOOOOOOOSHHH
The Doctor is IN
WHAT? I CAN'T HEAR YOU!!
BANG!
...ON YOUR HEAD.
I'M NOT SURE PIG IS A REAL DOCTOR.
IF ANYTHING, THE MUD ON MY HEAD IS MAKING ME SADDER.
HIC!
PIG! ARE YOU EVEN MEDICALLY TRAINED?
HIC!

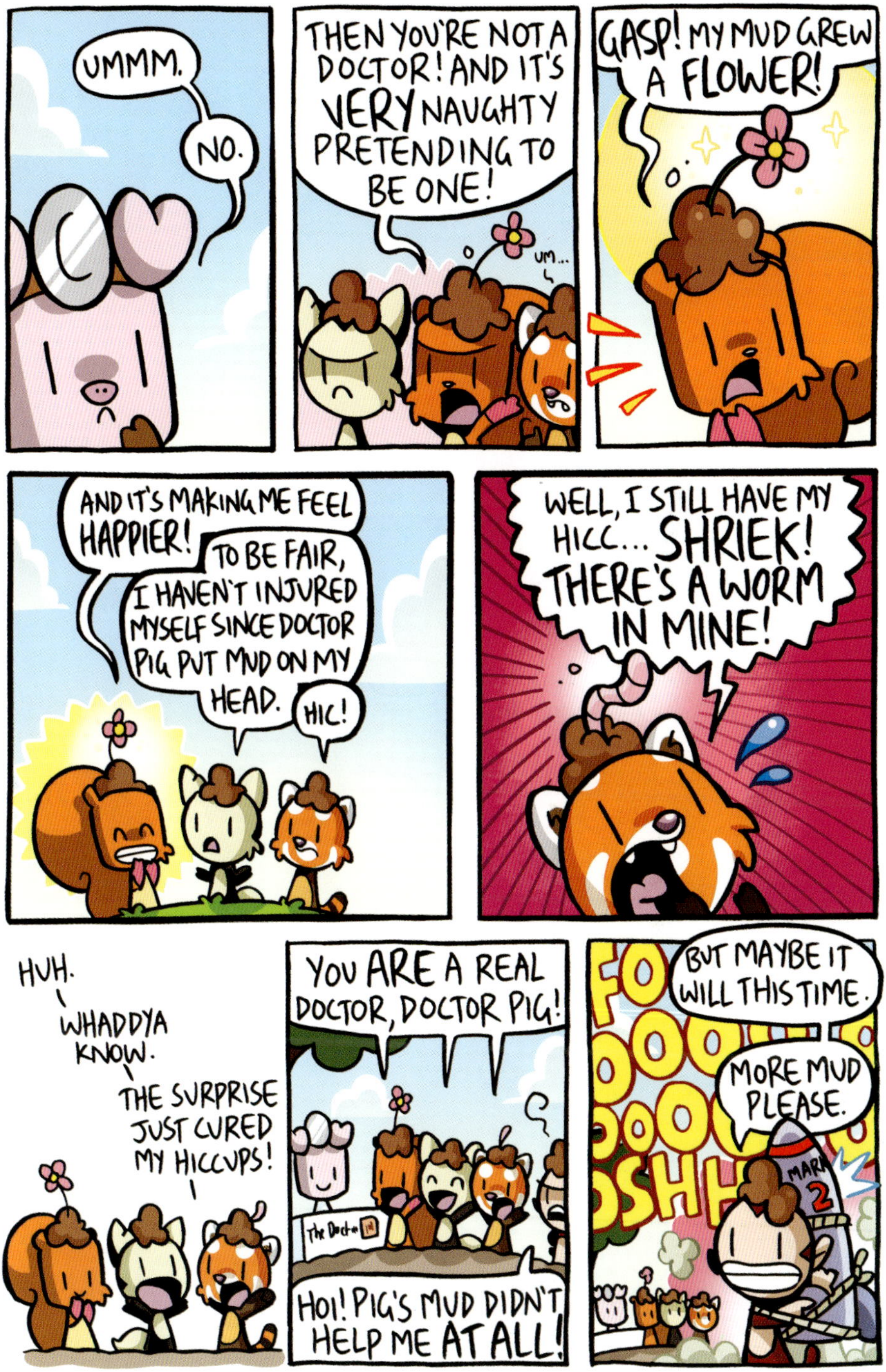
UMMM.
NO.
THEN YOU'RE NOT A DOCTOR! AND IT'S VERY NAUGHTY PRETENDING TO BE ONE!
UM...
GASP! MY MUD GREW A FLOWER!
AND IT'S MAKING ME FEEL HAPPIER!
TO BE FAIR, I HAVEN'T INJURED MYSELF SINCE DOCTOR PIG PUT MUD ON MY HEAD.
HIC!
WELL, I STILL HAVE MY HICC... SHRIEK! THERE'S A WORM IN MINE!
HUH.
WHADDYA KNOW.
THE SURPRISE JUST CURED MY HICCUPS!
YOU ARE A REAL DOCTOR, DOCTOR PIG!
The Doctor IN
HOI! PIG'S MUD DIDN'T HELP ME AT ALL!
BUT MAYBE IT WILL THIS TIME.
MORE MUD PLEASE.

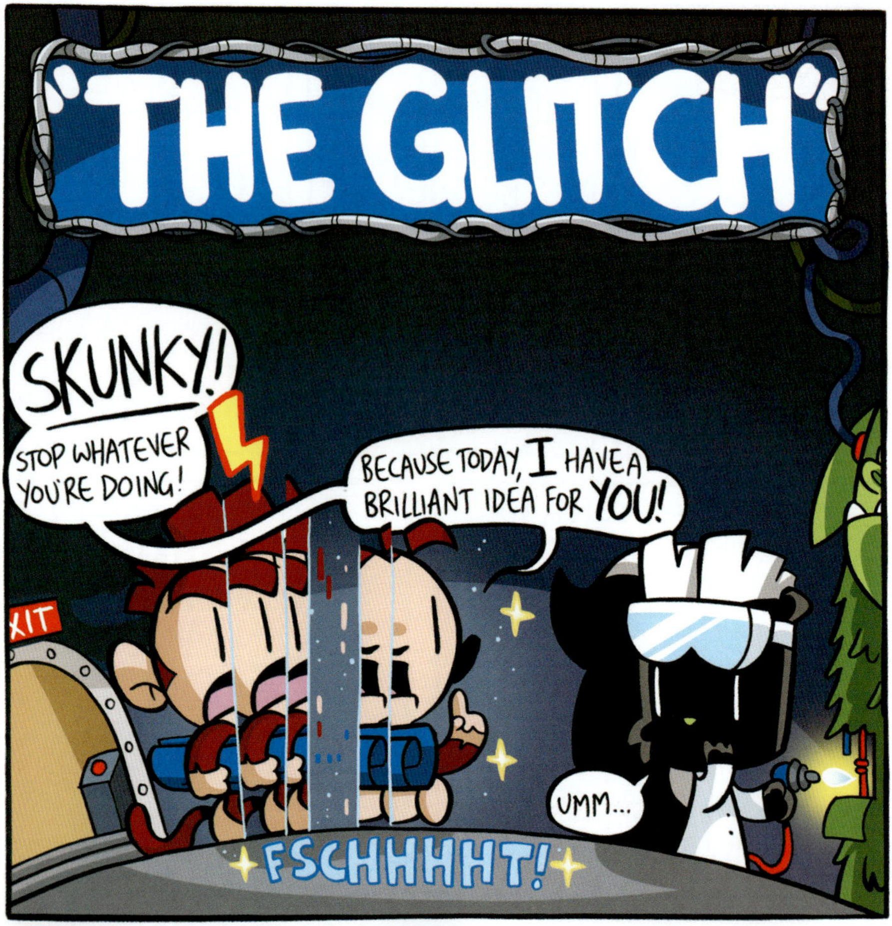
"THE GLITCH"
SKUNKY!
STOP WHATEVER YOU'RE DOING!
BECAUSE TODAY, I HAVE A BRILLIANT IDEA FOR YOU!
XIT
UMM...
FSCHHHHT!

MONKEY, DID YOU JUST... GLITCH?
BEHOLD, YOUR NEXT INVENTION!
Idea! ROBOT SNAKES
I MIGHT NEED A BIT MORE DETAIL THAN THIS.

OH C'MON, DO I HAVE TO DO EVERYTHIIII
IIIIIIIIIIIIIIIIIIIII
NOW YOU'RE BUFFERING!
HOW VERY DARE YOU!
ARE YOU... ARE YOU A ROBOT MONKEY? I DON'T REMEMBER BUILDING A ROBOT MONKEY!!
GLCKLE!
WHAT?
I'M NOT A ROBOT!
A ROBOT WOULD SAY THAT.
NYAH!
WELL, WOULD A ROBOT BE SMART ENOUGH TO...
...COME UP WITH A SECOND IDEA!
Idea 2
VAMPIRES
(somehow)

OH.
WAIT! YOU'RE GLITCHING TOO!
WELL, UM, YES.
FSCHT!
WE CAN'T ALL BE ROBOTS!
WE'RE NOT. SOMETHING IS VERY, VERY WRONG.
PANIC!
THE WHOLE WORLD IS STRUGGLING TO LOAD!
WHAT... WHAT DOES THAT MEAN?
PROGRESS
48%
IT MEANS SIMULATION THEORYYYYY.
I DON'T KNOW WHAT THAT IIIIIIIIIIIS.
ALL YOU NEED TO KNOW IS THAT WE'RE BEING WATCHED, AND I HAVE WAY TOO MANY SECRETS TO BE DISCOVERED.
EMERGENCY SHUTDOWN
YOU MIGHT WANT TO RUN AWAY SCREAMING.

CONNECTION LOST
BOOM!
NO! NO! DON'T CUT OUT NOW!
RRRGH! I'D FOUND IT! AFTER ALL THESE YEARS OF LOOKING, I'D FINALLY FOUND IT!
BUT THE WI-FI IN THIS APARTMENT IS TERRIBLE.
I SHOULDN'T HAVE EVEN TRIED.
SCHOOF!
I NEED TO GET BACK INTO THE OFFICE.
PLUG IN PROPERLY.
I...
I...

GLEEEE! I FOUND IT!
PLAY IT COOL, TOBY.
ACT NORMAL.
GET A COFFEE OR SOMETHING.
YUM YUM
PIZZA
WELCOME
TECH SHACK
COMPUTER REPAIRS
OPEN
AHEM! MORNING, DARYLL.
GRUNT.
I'LL, UH, BE OUT BACK IF ANYONE NEEDS ME.
GRUNT.
BEEP!

WHIRRR
WHIRRR
BEEP!
GOOD MORNING, TOBY.
MORNING, ALICE.
I TRUST YOU SLEPT WELL LAST NIGHT?
NEVER DO.
WHICH SIMULATION WOULD YOU LIKE TO RUN TODAY, TOBY?
A Lovely sunset
LOOSHKIN
It's MISTER FARTS!
SLURP

ALICE, YOU DO THIS JOKE EVERY DAY.
AND ONE DAY YOU'LL LAUGH AT IT, TOBY.
I WOULDN'T BET ON IT.
JUST RUN THE USUAL, IF YOU WOULD.
MONKEY
RUN PREVIOUS SIMULATIONS
YEAR 7 - MULTIVERSE MIX-UP
YEAR 8 - THE IMPOSSIBLE PIG
YEAR 9 - BUNNY BONANZA
WHICH YEAR WOULD YOU LIKE ME TO LOAD UP?
LET'S START THIS YEAR AGAIN. FROM THE BEGINNING.
OH.
ARE YOU SURE, TOBY?
I FOUND IT, ALICE. I FOUND THE GLITCH.

AND NOW I JUST NEED TO FIND IT AGAIN...
BUNNY VS MONKEY
AHHH.
WHAT A BEAUTIFULLY QUIET WINTER MORNING!
LET'S HOPE IT STAYS THAT WAY.
HEY BUNNY!
JUST CHECKING, DO YOU LIKE ROBOT VAMPIRE SNAKES?
UMM.. PROBABLY NOT.
YOU MIGHT WANNA
CLOSE YOUR EYES THEN!!
HEH HEH.
SLURP
FEELS LIKE THIS IS GOING TO BE A GOOD YEAR.

"UN-LUCKY"
SPONSORED BY SLOP!™
THE DRINK YOU MIGHT WANT TO WASH FIRST!
HWUARGH!! HUUUARGH!!
!!!
GET BACK, FOUL BEAST!
I KNOW THE SACRED ART OF HITTING THINGS WITH A BROOM!
WAIT! WAIT!
IT'S ME! LUCKY! THE LUCKIEST ANIMAL IN THE WOODS!
YOU KNOW, FOR THE LUCKIEST ANIMAL IN THE WOODS, YOU DON'T HAVE MUCH LUCK.
UGH! TELL ME ABOUT IT!

I WAS OUT FOR A WALK DRINKING A CAN OF DELICIOUS SLOP™...
SLURP!
...WHEN I WAS ATTACKED BY SKUNKY'S NEWEST INVENTION!
LOOK OUT, IT'S SOCKO (NAME STILL TO BE DECIDED UPON).
IT DRANK TOO MUCH SLOP™ AND SHORT-CIRCUITED.
IT'S JUST SHEER BAD LUCK YOU CAME THIS WAY!
MMM!
SLOP™
BIG CHUGGER EDITION.
SO YOU RAN AWAY AND FELL INTO A HEDGE?
WELL, NO...

I FELL INTO A TRAP LE FOX HAD DUG...
ARGH!
ZUT ALORS!
...AND THEN SOCKO FELL ON TOP OF ME!
FLUMP!
AH, BON!
BUT THEN HOW DID YOU GET THE JELLY ON YOUR HEAD?
OH, THAT...
WHEN I CRAWLED OUT OF THE TRAP, WEENIE THOUGHT I WAS A HEDGE MONSTER!
SHRIEK!
AND DROPPED HER JELLY ON ME!
I NEED A NICE, RELAXING CUP OF WARM SLOP™
OOH, THAT'S BETTER.
SLURP!
LUCKY, YOU HAVE HAD SUCH A BAD DAY! DO YOU KNOW WHAT YOU NEED?
N...NO?

LEGAL NOTICES: SLOP™ MAY CAUSE DIZZINESS, CHRONIC FLATULENCE AND, IN EXTREME CASES, YOU MAY GROW AN EXTRA NOSE. SLOP™ IS NOT TO BE CONSUMED, INSTEAD IT SHOULD BE USED TO CLEAN DRAINS. MAY BE FICTIONAL.

BEWARE THE
PUG OF DOOOM!
BWOOOO

IT CAN FART ITSELF INTO SPACE!
FRPPPPPPP!
ITS HEAD IS RADIO-CONTROLLED!
HUB-B-B-B-B-B-B-B-B-B-B-B-B-B-B
IT CAN LICK ITS OWN BOTTOM!
TOO RUDE!!
AND ALL IT NEEDS FOR POWER...
... IS A LONG EXTENSION LEAD...
...AND A HOUSEHOLD PLUG SOCKET!
HOI! DO YOU MIND?!

YES, THIS PUG OF DOOM CAN BE ALL YOURS FOR THE LOW PRICE OF NINE HUNDRED AND NINETY-NINE POUNDS!
UM...
UNPLUG YOUR DOG! I WANT TO WATCH BUNNY SHOWS!
I CAN'T DO THAT!
I HAVEN'T SHOWN PIG THE BEST BIT YET!
BOOP!
VMMMM

A GIANT NUCLEAR CORE!!
FOOSHH!
OR, AS WE CALL IT IN FRONT OF THE PUG...
...THE BALLY BALL-BALL!
GNAW! GNAW! GNAW!
SKUNKY! WHAT ARE YOU DOING? IF THAT PUG CHOMPS TOO HARD, WE COULD ALL BE BLOWN SKY HIGH!
SCOOT! SCOOT! SCOOT!
PAT PAT!
AWW, HE'S JUST PLAYING. ISN'T HE? ISN'T HE?
SO, PIG! WHADDYA SAY? FANCY A NEW PET?
I... I...

CLUNK!
CHOMP!
PSCHH!
BUNNY SHOWS!
SCHHH
A NUCLEAR WINTER!
SCHHHHHHH
I THINK I'LL GET A HAMSTER!

"PIGGY POG POG"
RUN IN FEAR, FOOLISH CREATURES! FOR YOU ARE ABOUT TO EXPERIENCE THE TERROR THAT IS THE...
PIGGY POG POG!!
WOO!
BOOM!
BOOM!
BOOM!

METAL STEVE, THIS DOES NOT COMPUTE. WHAT IS ENJOYABLE ABOUT SUCH RELENTLESS DESTRUCTION?
WOO!!
MY HEAD'S ON FIRE!
MY BUM'S ON FIRE!
BZZT!
HEE HEE!
CURIOUS.

MONKEY! THIS IS ONE BATTLE YOU SHALL NOT WIN!
BECAUSE WE HAVE OUR OWN PIGGY POG POG!!
HUH?
POGGY POOG... POOG?
RELEASE THE POOG!
P-TWAN
I DIDN'T FINISH MY SANDWIIIIIICH!
OH, HELLO!
SCRE
OMP!!
HAR HAR!

BZZT! CHOMP!
BUT... BUT THAT IS NOT FUNNY.
THE FIRST PIG ATE THE SECOND PIG. THAT COULD BE VERY DANGEROUS.
WOO!
WE SHOULD NOT BE ENJOYING THIS, OR ENCOURAGING IT. HIGH-RISK SCENARIOS SUCH AS THIS SEEM TO ARISE EVERY DAY IN THESE WOODS!
PRRPP PPPPP!
WHEEE, BISCUITS!

AND YET, EVERYONE ALWAYS SEEMS OKAY.
FLO-MP!
WE ALWAYS WAKE UP COMPLETELY UNSCATHED.
FARTING OUT YOUR PIG DEFLATED MY PIGGY POG POG AND NOW EVERYTHING'S ON FIRE!!
WOO!
WOO!!

"JOURNEY FOR THE WOBBLEBERRIES"
OH NO, IT'S A DISASTER! A DISASTER!
WHAT IS IT, WEENIE? IS YOUR KITCHEN ON FIRE?
OH, THAT.
PFFT.
THAT'S NORMAL.
NO, IT'S PIG'S BIRTHDAY TODAY, AND I'M TRYING TO BAKE HIM A SPECIAL WOBBLEBERRY CAKE...
...BUT I'VE RUN OUT OF WOBBLEBERRIES!
A...
WOBBLE...
WHU WHU?

WOBBLEBERRIES ARE DELICIOUS, BUT THEY'RE ALSO EXCEEDINGLY RARE!
MAYBE I COULD HELP YOU FIND SOME?
WOULD YOU? HERE, YOU'LL NEED SOME SUPPLIES!
FLUMP!
FORTUNATELY, I HAVE A MAP OF WHERE TO FIND THE TASTIEST, PLUMPEST WOBBLEBERRIES OF ALL!!
THEY'RE UP THERE!
OF COURSE THEY ARE.

MIND OUT FOR THE ROCKFALLS!
YES, THANK YOU.
AND THE SWARMING GNATS!
NYAH!
NYAH!
AND THE ANGRY GOAT!!
IT DOESN'T LOOK VERY ANGR...
SCREEE
HOO BOY, AND THIS IS ONLY PAGE ONE OF THE MAP. WAIT TILL YOU SEE WHAT'S ON PAGE SEVENTEEN!
MAP
PHOOEY TO ALL THIS, I CAN'T GO ANY FURTHER!
BEH!
MAYBE INSTEAD I COULD JUST USE A LITTLE WOODLAND MAGIC...

...AND CREATE MY OWN WOBBLEBERRIES DOWN HERE!
RTHDAY
PIG!
BUT IT...IT'S NOT MY BIRTHDAY.
IT IS NOW.
RTHDAY
PIG!
CHOMP! CHOMP! CHOMP!

"BIG ME"
GOOD MORNING, EVERYONE!
SHRIEK!
WHAT ARE YOU ALL DOING? THAT LOOKS FUN.
UMM...
WE... WE'RE MAKING PAPER DOLL CHAINS!
OH. WE ARE?
OH, LET ME HAVE A GO, OH POO, OH CURSE MY BIG DAFT HANDS!
CRUSH! RIP!

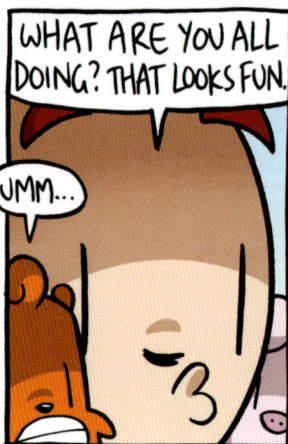

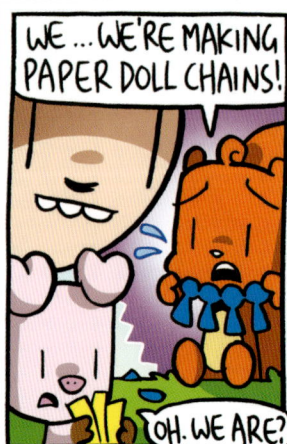

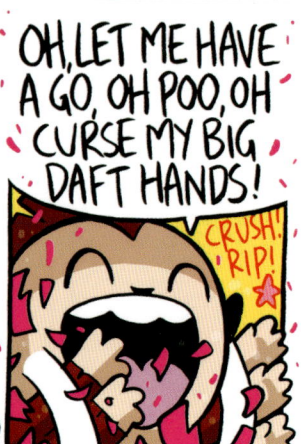

EE HEE HEE!
MONKEY, YOU SEEM... BIGGER.
I ASKED SKUNKY TO MAKE ME A ME COSTUME!
SIZE DEMANDS RESPECT!
DON'T TELL ME YOU WANT ONE TOO?
HAHA! WHO'S THE BIGGER BUNNY NOW?
IT'S ME. I'M A BUNNY.
GASP!
STOMP! STOMP! STOMP!

OH, FOR GOODNESS' SAKE.
NICE TRY, BUNNY, BUT I JUST WENT ONE BIGGER!
BIGGER THAN WHO?
ARGH!
I'M WORKING AS FAST AS I CAN!

TAA-DAA! BIG ME!
HMM. BIG-ISH.
GAH!
WHAT ARE WE ALL DOING?
IT DOESN'T MATTER ANY MORE!
NO, THIS IS GETTING VERY SILLY NOW. THE GAME'S OVER.

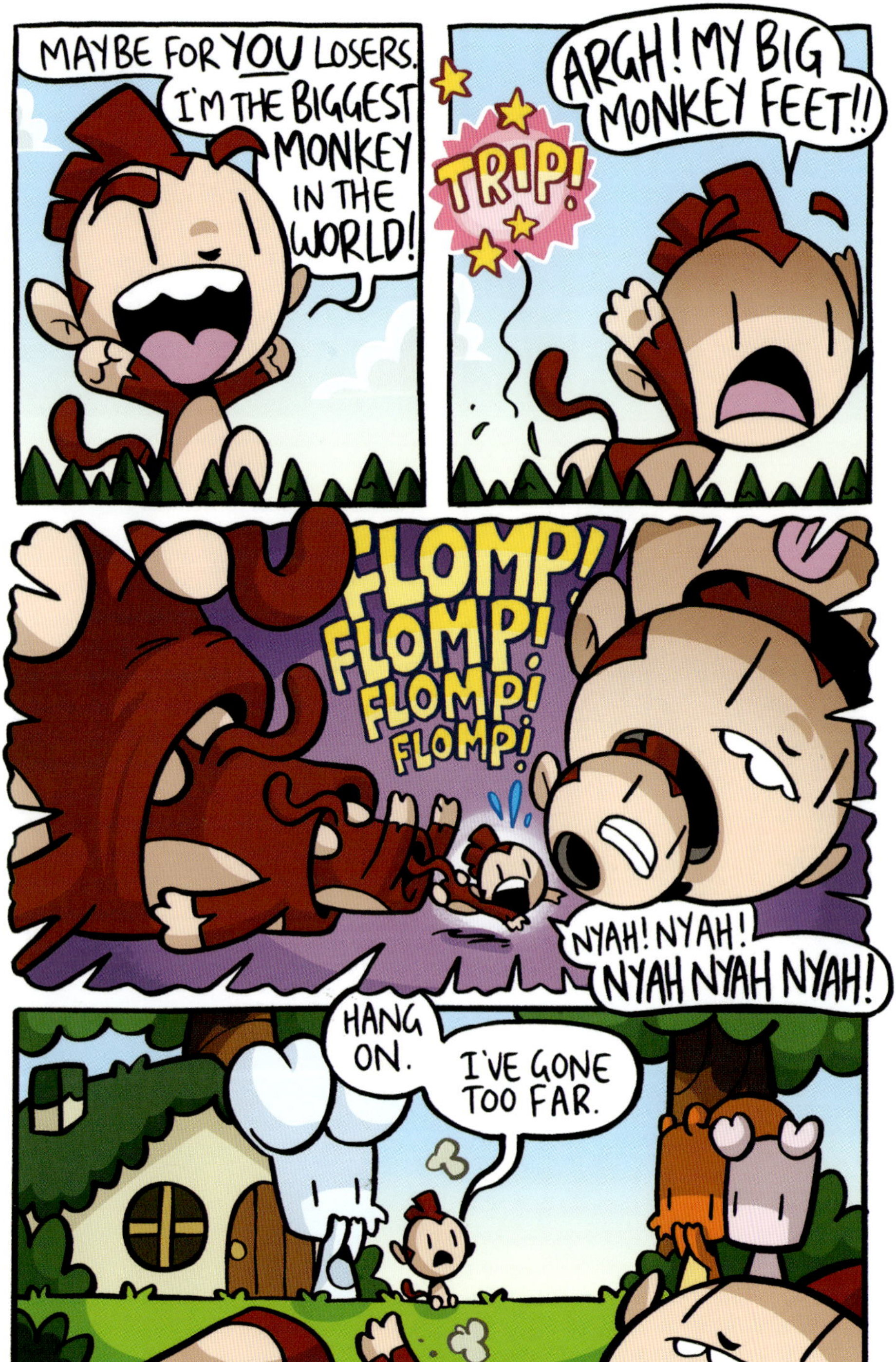
MAYBE FOR YOU LOSERS.
I'M THE BIGGEST MONKEY IN THE WORLD!
TRIP!
ARGH! MY BIG MONKEY FEET!!
FLOMP! FLOMP! FLOMP! FLOMP!
NYAH! NYAH! NYAH NYAH NYAH!
HANG ON.
I'VE GONE TOO FAR.

"BLOBLEMS"
BLOBBOBBOB
BOBBOB
WHO'S THERE?
BUNNY! I'VE MADE A TERRIBLE MISTAKE!
M...MONKEY?
WHAT ARE YOU DOING IN THERE?

SKUNKY CREATED AN ALL-CONSUMING GELATINOUS BLOB TO HELP ME TAKE OVER THE WOODS.
BUT THEN IT ATE ME!!
HAHA! WELL, CAN'T YOU JUST ASK SKUNKY TO PULL YOU OUT OF IT?
NOT REALLY...
HELLO!
PFFT! YOU TWO MADE THIS MESS, YOU CAN JUST FIX IT BY YOURSELVES.
BLOBBOBBOBBO
OH, FOR GOODNESS' SAKE.
THE BLOB WILL NOT STOP! ITS RAVENOUS APPETITE WILL NEVER BE SATED!!

MMM! CHEESE STICKS!
!
BLOBBBBOBBO
BOBBOBBOBBOBBOBBOBBOBBOBB
WELL, YOU'VE FINALLY DONE IT, SKUNKY.
YOU'VE INVENTED SOMETHING TOTALLY CATASTROPHIC!
BZZP!
IN FACT, I THINK THIS THING HAS SWALLOWED EVERYONE EXCEPTTT...
...ACTION BEAVER!!
GLARP!

WELL, DUH!
WE NEEDED SOMEONE TO CONTROL THIS THING.
WHAT?
PSYCHIC REMOTE-CONTROL HELMET!
WHAT ACTION BEAVER DECIDES, THE BLOB DOES!
BEEP!
BOOP BOOP!
BUT ACTION BEAVER IS A NONSENSE! WHY WOULD YOU ENTRUST IT TO HIM?
BECAUSE... AT 3P.M. EVERY AFTERNOON, ACTION BEAVER HAS A NAP...
ZZNCK
...CAUSING THE BLOB TO COLLAPSE!!

A BUILT-IN FAILSAFE, IN CASE THINGS GO WRONG.
HUH. THAT IS KINDA CLEVER.
THE ONLY THING THAT WOKE HIM UP LAST TIME WAS ME HONKING THIS HORN.
HONKKK!
SNCKKK!
OH NO.
OH N...
BLOBBBBBBB
WHY, MONKEY? WHYYYYY?!
I MADE ANOTHER TERRIBLE MISTAKE! WHEEEE!!
OBBOBB
BLOBBOBBOU

"JELLY PLOPS"
GASP! MONKEY?!
NOT MONKEY!! YOU SHALL REFER TO ME-BZZT-AS...
JELLY PLOPS!
I AM A -BZZT- ROBOT, DESIGNED TO SHOOT JELLY WITH PINPOINT ACCURACY!
THPT
YOU'RE NOT A ROBOT, YOU'RE JUST MONKEY IN A SILLY COSTUME!
I AM NOT!
YEAH, YOU ARE.

WOULD A MONKEY IN A COSTUME FILL YOUR HOUSE WITH JELLY?
BOILP!
YES!
ALSO, ARGH!
STOP BEING SO SILLY, MONKEY! THAT'S GOING TO TAKE FOREVER TO CLEAN UP!
NO NEED! BZZT! BECAUSE I MAKE MY JELLY WITH...
TH-BOOM!
...FIZZY WATER!!
ARGH!

NYAH HA HAA! EVERYONE RUN IN FEAR! JELLYPLOPS IS-BZZT-BLOWING UP THE WOODS WITH HIS HIGHLY VOLATILE JELLY!
BPTH
BOOM!
BOOM
I DON'T KNOW WHAT'S GOING ON, BUT I BROUGHT CRISPS FOR US TO EAT WHILE IT'S HAPPENING.
FLOMP
THH-
BOOM!

MY CRISPS! YOU'VE GOT JELLY ON THEM!
CHOMP!
OH, HANG ON, THAT'S... DELICIOUS!!
YUM! CRISPS AND JELLY!
OOH, THEY'RE VERY MOREISH!
CHOMP! CHOMP! CHOMP!
!!
STOP IT! BZZT! STOP MAKING THE BEST OF A BAD SITUATION!
HOP! HOP! HOP!
UMM... JELLYPLOPS? DIDN'T YOU SAY YOUR JELLY WAS HIGHLY VOLATILE?
FIZZ!
POP!
OH...
POP!
...JELLYPLOPS!
NYAHHHHHH
TH-BOOM!
WHAT'S GOING ON?
WHO WAS THAT HANDSOME ROBOT?

'THE SECOND GLITCH'
WHAT IS...
...THE MOON?
WELL, METAL EVE, THE MOON IS A BIG LUMP OF ROCK... SORT OF... FLOATING IN SPACE.
I THINK.
HEE HEE! THAT'S SILLY, BUNNY!
WHAT IS THE MOON THEN, WEENIE?

WHY, IT'S A BIG LUMP OF CHEESE! EVERYONE KNOWS THAT.
CHOMP!
SOMETIMES I CAN SEE A FACE IN THE MOON.
A FACE?
SOMETIMES I CAN HEAR IT TALKING.
IT SINGS LITTLE SONGS.
WHAT?
YOU'RE ALL WRONG! THE MOON IS MY OFF-WORLD LABORATORY, CURRENTLY BEING PILOTED BY MONKEY.
PLAN
BRUM!
WHAT IS?
MONKEY! IF YOU'RE HERE, THEN WHO'S DRIVING THE MOON?
PLAN
BRUM!

LE FOX, DO YOU KNOW WHAT THE MOON IS?
BIEN SUR!
ZE MOON IS A GIANT SPOTLIGHT, AND SUPERIOR BEINGS OBSERVE US FROM BEHIND IT!
NO ONE WANTS TO HEAR ZE TRUTH.
I'M TELLING YOU, IT'S MADE OF CHEESE!
THEN WHY DOESN'T IT SMELL?
LOOK! THERE'S THE FACE!!

HELLO, MISTER MOON!
ALICE, CAN THEY... CAN THEY SEE ME?
THAT SHOULD NOT BE POSSIBLE, TOBY.
SO WHY...
...IS THE PIG WAVING AT ME?
COOEE!
UNLESS...

IT'S HAPPENING AGAIN! ALICE! WE'VE FOUND IT!!
THE GLITCH?
THE GLITCH! THE SOFTWARE ANOMALY THAT HAS BEEN THINNING THE VEIL BETWEEN OUR WORLD AND THEIRS!
THE POINT AT WHICH BUNNY VS MONKEY STARTS TO SPILL INTO OUR WORLD!!
TEE HEE! YOU'RE FUNNY, MISTER MOON.
GASP! YOU KNOW WHAT THIS MEANS, DON'T YOU?
N... NO?
IT MEANS SIMULATION THEORYYYY!!
STILL NO.

YOU COULD JUST SAY THANK YOU, LE FOX, YOU WERE RIGHT ALL ALONG.
NO TIME! TOO MANY SECRETS TO DESTROY!
I CALCULATE SKUNKY WILL BE THE ONE TO WIDEN THE ANOMALY.
DEFINITELY. HE'LL PROBABLY WORK ALL OF THIS OUT SOONER OR LATER.
SECRET LAIR
WE CAN'T LET THAT HAPPEN. WE MUST FIND OUT WHAT'S CAUSING ALL THIS.
ZZZZ
RESTART THE YEAR!
WHAT, AGAIN?
AGAIN!
WE'RE NARROWING IT DOWN EACH TIME.
BOOM

AND THIS TIME...
...I'M GOING IN.
BUNNY VS MONKEY
IT SURE IS A COLD JANUARY, MISTER MOON.
I'VE NOT BEEN UP TO MUCH.
I PUT SOME CUSTARD ON MY HEAD.
NOT ON PURPOSE, THOUGH.
WHAT ARE YOU DOING, PIG?
OH! JUST TALKING TO THE MOON.
WHAT IS...
...THE MOON?

THE MOON IS MY FRIEND! I TELL IT ALL ABOUT MY DAY.
AND THEN IT WATCHES OVER ME WHILE I WALK HOME.
THE MOON KEEPS ME SAFE.
NOTHING IS SCARY WHILE THE MOON IS OUT.
BIP BIP!
BPP-BOOP!
FZZ!
PARK WARDEN
DOWNLOADING AVATAR: PARK WARDEN

AHH...
I'VE NOT BEEN IN THIS SKIN FOR A WHILE.
CAN YOU HEAR ME, ALICE?
LOUD AND CLEAR, TOBY.
K WARDEN
GOOD, THEN LET'S GET STARTED.
WE'RE GOING TO FIND THE GLITCH FROM THE INSIDE.
HISSSSS! WEIRD HUMAN! WATCH ME DRESS UP LIKE A VAMPIRE AND SCARE PIG WITH RUBBER SNAKES!
HMM.
MAYBE A TEA FIRST.
K WARDEN
SCREEAM
SAVE US, MOON! SAVE US!

"ROLL 'EM UP!"
A NEW YEAR, AND THE WEATHER IS JUST STARTING TO WARM UP...
...JUST IN TIME FOR CHEESY BUGS* TO COME OUT OF HIBERNATION!
SHRIEK!!

*ALSO KNOWN AS: SLATERS, GRANNYGREYS, PILLBUGS, CHEESYBOBS, ROLY POLIES, CHUCKYPIGS, OR WOODLICE!

HANG ON, I DON'T REMEMBER CHEESYBUGS BEING THIS BIG.
HI, BUNNY!
COO-EE!

THIS IS A ROBOT CHEESYBUG. SKUNKY INVENTED IT!
CONTROL PANEL
WE BOUGHT IT OFF HIM!

WHY WOULD SKUNKY SELL AN INVENTION?
HE'S SELLING ALL OF THEM!
CLIMB ON, WE'LL SHOW YOU!
IS...IS THIS THING GOING TO TAKE US THERE?
HER NAME IS BARBARA.
WHUP!!
YEARGH!
AND SHE'S THE FASTEST CHEESYBUG IN THE WORLD!
VOOOOOOOOOOOOOOOOOOOM!

SCREE EEEE ECH!
OHHH, NO.
NO RETURNS.
BARBARA'S YOURS NOW.
YARD SALE
UNLESS, OF COURSE, YOU'VE COME BACK FOR MORE BARGAINS!
HOW ABOUT A NUCLEAR WARHEAD?
NEVER BEEN USED.
DO YOU HAVE IT IN BLUE?
SPLPTBH!
A JELLYHAT!
IT'S YOURS FOR TWO ACORNS AND A PEANUT!
I ONLY HAVE SOME JELLY.
SOLD!
HEY, WHAT DOES THIS DO?
THAT'S THE REMOTE CONTROL FOR MY SATELLITE LASER SYSTEM.
WELL, IT TASTES BORING.
HOMP! CHOMP! CHOMP!
CHOOM!!
SOLD!

SKUNKY, WHY ARE YOU SELLING OFF YOUR LIFE'S WORK?
DO YOU KNOW, I CAN'T EXPLAIN IT...
I JUST HAVE THIS REALLY WEIRD FEELING THAT I NEED TO GET RID OF MY SECRETS.
HOW MUCH FOR ACTION BEAVER?
OH, HE'S FREE.
SOLD!
HE HONKS A LOT, THOUGH.
HONK!
SCREE!
GRUARGHHH!
SCREAM! BARBARA'S OUT OF CONTROL!!
OH, YEAH, SHE'S DEFECTIVE.
EVERYTHING HERE IS DEFECTIVE!!
SQUEAL!
BOOM!
SPLPTH!
HONK!
I'M HARDLY GOING TO GET RID OF THE COOL STUFF, AM I?
OOF!

MINE
MINE
MINE
MINE
MINE
MINE
OH!
WHAT A LOVELY FLOWER!
MINE
MINE
MINE
MINE
MINE
MINE
MINE
CAN'T HAVE THAT! THAT IS...
...MINE!!
MINE
MONKEY, WHAT ARE YOU DOING?

WELL, SINCE YOU WON'T LET ME TAKE OVER THE WOODS...
...I'M JUST CLAIMING EVERYTHING IN IT AS MINE INSTEAD.
I CAN DO THAT. IT'S THE LAW.
LAW? WHAT LAW SAYS YOU CAN JUST WRITE 'MINE' ON THINGS?
THE LAW IN MY HEAD.
MINE
THIS IS CRAZY! NONE OF THE OTHER ANIMALS WILL STAND FOR THIS!
BIT LATE FOR THAT.
HELLO, BUNNY!
WE'RE MONKEYS!
OOK OOK!
MINE
MINE
MINE
MINE

NO, YOU'RE MONKEY'S.
MONKEYS!
MONKEY'S. THERE'S AN APOSTROPHE.
OOK OOK!
NEVER MIND. THE POINT IS, I OWN EVERYTHING NOW. IT'S ALL...
MINE
...MINE!!
PLAP!
MINE
NOW YOU... ARE MINE.
WHAT? HANG ON.
MINE
WHICH MEANS EVERYTHING THAT IS YOURS ... IS NOW MINE TOO!
THIS ISN'T FAIR! THIS ISN'T THE LAW!
MINE
MINE
MINE
IT'S THE LAW IN MY HEAD.
MINE
RRRGHH!

WE'RE BUNNIES NOW.
RIBBIT RIBBIT.
WELL, BUNNIES DON'T GO RIBBIT RIBBIT, BUT IF YOU WANTED TO DO SOMETHING FOR ME...
MINE
MINE
MINE
...YOU COULD TAKE ALL THESE STICKERS OFF EVERYTHING!
FLING!
THE WOODS DON'T BELONG TO ANYONE!
MINE
MINE
MINE
MINE
HAR HAR!
I'M FREE!
MINE

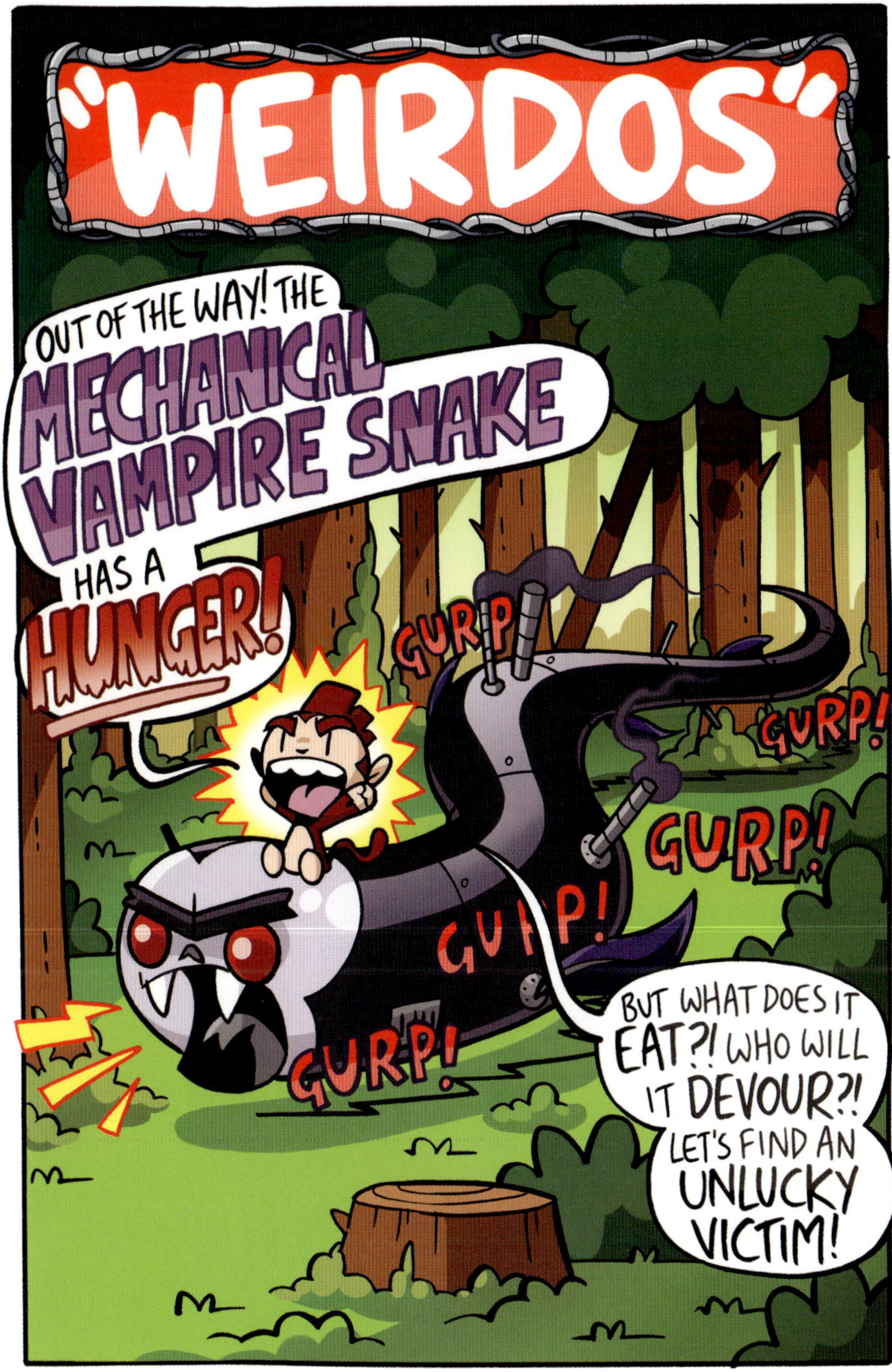
"WEIRDOS"
OUT OF THE WAY! THE MECHANICAL VAMPIRE SNAKE HAS A HUNGER!
GURP
GURP!
GURP!
GURP!
GURP!
BUT WHAT DOES IT EAT?! WHO WILL IT DEVOUR?! LET'S FIND AN UNLUCKY VICTIM!

PARK WARD
NOTICES
AHH. WHAT A BEAUTIFUL, PERFECTLY RENDERED MORNING.
VOOOOM!!
NOPE!
SHRIEK!
NOT YOU.
GURP!
VAMPIRE... SNAKE? THAT FEELS STRANGELY...
GURP! GURP! GURP
...FAMILIAR?
SHRIEK!
INDEED. I, TOO, AM EXPERIENCING WHAT YOU MIGHT CALL DÉJÀ VU.

IN FACT, I CALCULATE A 23% SIMILARITY TO EVENTS WHICH SHOULD BE IN MY MEMORY BANKS, BUT WHICH ARE CURRENTLY INACCESSIBLE.
BZZ!
WHIRR!
YOU... YOU'RE THE ROBOT BEAR SKUNKY BUILT.
CORRECT.
BUT I HAVE NO RECORD OF YOU.
M...ME? WELL, I'M THE PARK WARDEN.
IT'S MY JOB TO WATCH OVER THE WOODLANDS IN CASE ANYTHING WEIRD HAPPENS.
DEFINE 'WEIRD'.
ACTUALLY, SINCE YOU'RE HERE, PERHAPS YOU COULD HELP ME. YOU COULD OBSERVE THE OTHER ANIMALS UP CLOSE, AND REPORT BACK IF YOU SEE ANYTHING... UNUSUAL.
WEIRD STUFF:
OOH! A PURPOSE!
I'VE BEEN LOOKING FOR ONE OF THOSE!
WEIRD STUFF:
REMEMBER, ANYTHING OUT OF THE ORDINARY!
I SHALL TRY MY BEST!

WUB
WUB
WUB
WUB
NO.
FOOOSH!
NO.
NOPE.
BZZZAP!
NO.
NO.
HMM.
NO.
HERE ARE MY FINDINGS.
I WOULD CALL THIS A NORMAL TUESDAY.

WELL, THIS IS GREAT. THANK YOU, EVE!
I'LL GO BACK TO MY HUT, AND READ IT ALL THR...
...AUGH!!
HUTS! IT EATS HUTS!!
GURP
GURP
GURP!
URP!
OKAY. THAT'S A BIT WEIRD.

"WHEN IN ROME"
CITIZENS, HAIL! YOUR GLORIOUS LEADER, EMPEROR MONKEYUS MAXIMUS III OF MONKEYOPIA COMMANDS YOUR LOYALTY, SERVITUDE AND POSH BISCUITS IF YOU HAVE ANY.
MONKEYPIA
OH, GO AWAY.
SLAM!
BAM! BAM! BAM! BAM! BAM! BA
NOW WHO CAN THAT BE?

CITIZEN BUNNY! YOU'RE UNDER ARREST FOR BEING VERY RUDE.
UNDER ARREST? PAH! I'D LIKE TO SEE YOU TRY AND ARREST ME!
SOME ARRESTING LATER...
HUH. FAIR ENOUGH. WHAT NOW?
NOW, YOU FACE MONKEYOPIAN JUSTICE!!
PUTT PUTT!
YOU MUST FIGHT FOR YOUR LIFE... IN THE COLOSSEUM!
THAT'S... JUST A BOX.
I DIDN'T HAVE TIME TO BUILD A COLOSSEUM, ALL RIGHT?
NEW PANTS
COLOSSEUM
I'M VERY BUSY.

WELL, OKAY, I'M IN.
AND NOW, YOUR OPPONENT! MONKEYOPIA'S MOST FEARSOME CREATURE OF LEGEND...
NEW PANTS COLOSSEUM
...THE STEVE-O-TAUR!!!
BAROOOOOO
THAT...THAT'S METAL STEVE'S HEAD...
...BUT WHERE'S THE REST OF HIM?!
OH, HIS BODY'S FINE. IT'S READING A BOOK.
UMM...
OKAY, LOSERS, NOW FIGHT!

HOLD ON, STEVE, WE COULD WORK TOGETHER, ESCAPE THIS BOX AS A TEAM!
ACTUALLY, FORGET IT.
?
WHIZZZ
I HAVE A STEW IN THE OVEN.
BOOT
PHEEEP!
BAROOOOO
I NEED TO GET HOME!

YOU KICKED HIS BUM AND HIS HEAD CAME OFF.
I DID.
CAN I GO NOW?
S'POSE SO.
THANK YOU.
BAROOO
A BIT LATER...
YOU! YOU'RE UNDER ARREST FOR BEING A PIG!
OKAY!
SKUNKY, STICK THE COLOSSEUM BACK TOGETHER.

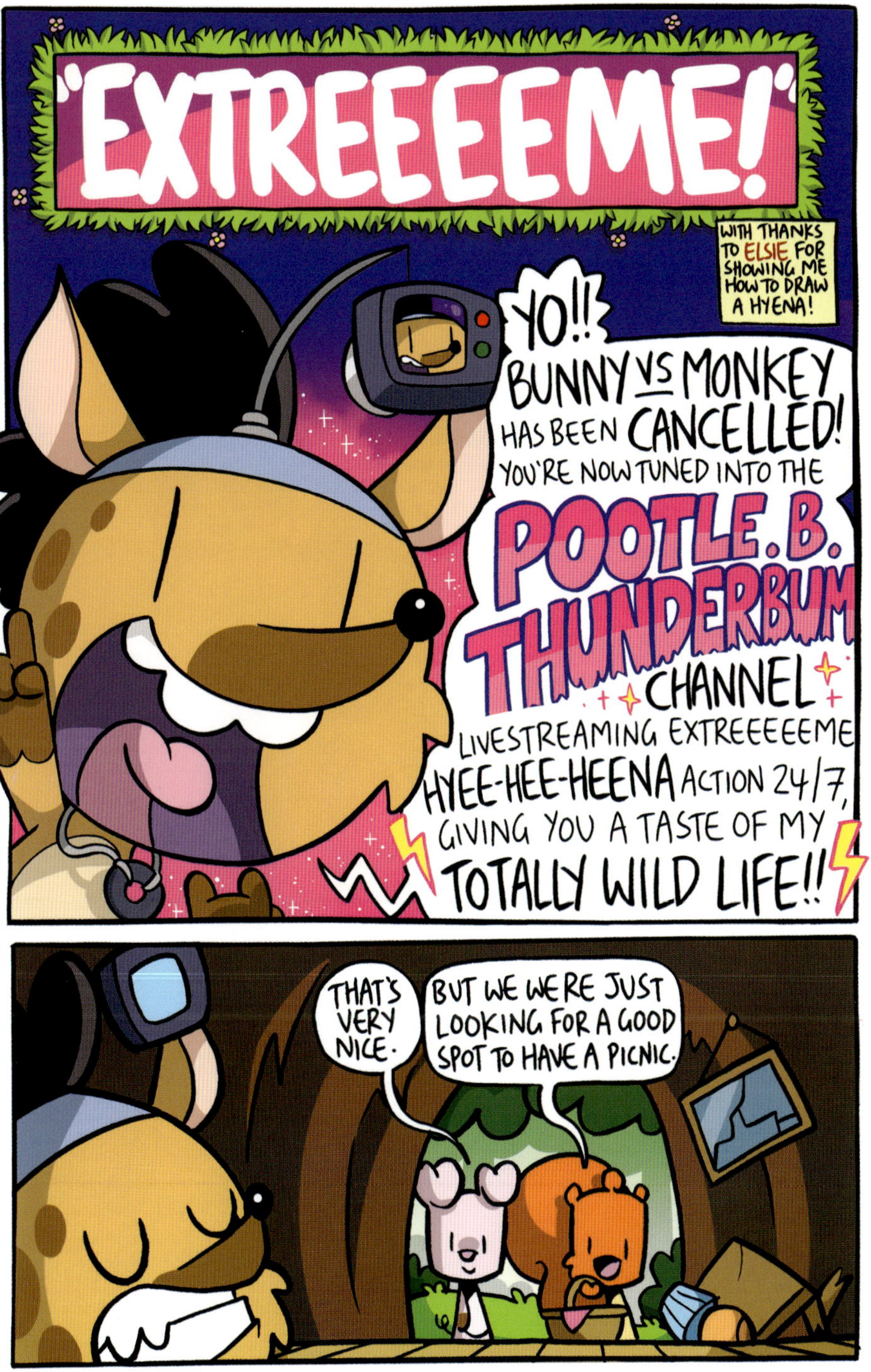
"EXTREEEEEME!"
WITH THANKS TO ELSIE FOR SHOWING ME HOW TO DRAW A HYENA!
YO!! BUNNY VS MONKEY HAS BEEN CANCELLED! YOU'RE NOW TUNED INTO THE POOTLE. B. THUNDERBUM CHANNEL LIVESTREAMING EXTREEEEEEME HYEE-HEE-HEENA ACTION 24/7, GIVING YOU A TASTE OF MY TOTALLY WILD LIFE!!
THAT'S VERY NICE.
BUT WE WERE JUST LOOKING FOR A GOOD SPOT TO HAVE A PICNIC.

A GOOD SPOT? WELL, I HAPPEN TO KNOW THE FRESHEST PEAKS!
OH YAY!
BUT TO GET THERE, WE'LL HAVE TO GO EXTREEEEEME!
WINK!
OKAY!
UMM...
PARKOUR!!
PARKING!
I...I'M NOT SURE THIS IS A GOOD IDEA.
HEY! I HEAR YOU GUYS LIKE... PICNICS!
YEAH!
WE TOLD YOU THAT.
WELL, HAVE YOU EVER TRIED...
PLUCK!

PARKOUR!
PARKOUR!
PARKOUR!
CACTUS PATCH
CHOMP!
...EXTREME PICNICKING!!
I WANNA!
PIG, NO. THAT LOOKS VERY VERY...
...DANGEROUS.

OUCH!
OUCH!
OUCH!
OUCH!
OUCH!
CRUMP!
I CHANGED MY MIND! I CHANGED MY MIIIIIND!
SIGH.
HOP!
SPIN!
FLIP!
LEAP
YOU'RE A VERY SILLY PIG.
SORRY.
GRAB!

WHOA, DUDES! THAT WAS LIKE, INTENSE!
DO IT AGAIN!
YOU'RE AN IDIOT.
SHOVE!
ARGH!
YO, OUR CACTUS VID WENT VIRAL! WHAT CAN WE DO TO TOP IT?
NOTHING.
GO AWAY.
OKAY!
PARKOUR!

"AND NOW, A SPECIAL PRESENTATION"
THIS COMIC FEATURES EXCLUSIVE + LUCK + TECHNOLOGY!
LUCKY!
YOU CAN NOW FOLLOW LUCKY'S JOURNEY WITH THE FORTUNE-O-METER!
UNLUCKY!
LUCKY, THE UNLUCKIEST RED PANDA IN THE WORLD!
IT'S A LONG STORY.

OH! ACTION BEAVER!
MAYBE YOU CAN HELP ME GET FREE?
LUCKY!

UNLUCKY!
GRMPHMPHLE.
FZZZZZZ
ZZZZ
OH, JUST MY L...
...UCKKK!!
BOOOOM!
COUGH! SPLUTTER!
WELL, WOULD YOU LOOK AT THAT... I'M FREE!
LUCKY!
AND THERE'S SOMETHING EMBEDDED INTO THE REMAINS OF THE BOULDER.
LUCKY!
GASP! THE FOSSILISED REMAINS OF A FLOPTAEOPTERYX DINOSAUR!
A... WHAT?

THESE ARE VERY RARE. YOU'RE INCREDIBLY LUCKY TO FIND ONE!
M...ME? LUCKY?
LUCKY!
AND EVEN LUCKIER, I HAPPEN TO BE CARRYING MY LATEST INVENTION...THE PORTABLE
GLOOP!
DINO REVIVO 5000!
THIS DEVICE WILL RESEQUENCE THE FOSSIL'S D.N.A. AND THEN BRING IT... BACK TO LIFE!
DING!
AH! IT'S DONE!
GLARK!!
B...BUT I THOUGHT IT WOULD HAVE FLESH! AND SKIN!
WHY? SKELETONS ARE AWESOME!
UNLUCKY!
GLOMP!
SHRIEK!
AW, IT THINKS YOU'RE ITS MUMMY! YOU'RE SO LUCKY!
GO AND ENJOY SOME TIME TOGETHER, YOU TWO!
OW! OW! OW!

UNLUCKY!
OW!
OW!
OW!
OW!
UNLUCKY!
OW!
OW OW!
OW!
UNLUCKY!
OW.
OW.
OW.
GLMPH!
ACTION BEAVER! I DON'T SUPPOSE YOU KNOW HOW I CAN GET THIS THING OFF MY HEAD?
UNLUCKY!
...NO, WAIT...
LUCKY!
GRMPHMPHLE.
TNT
BOOOOO OOOM!!
I REALLY NEED A DAY OFF.

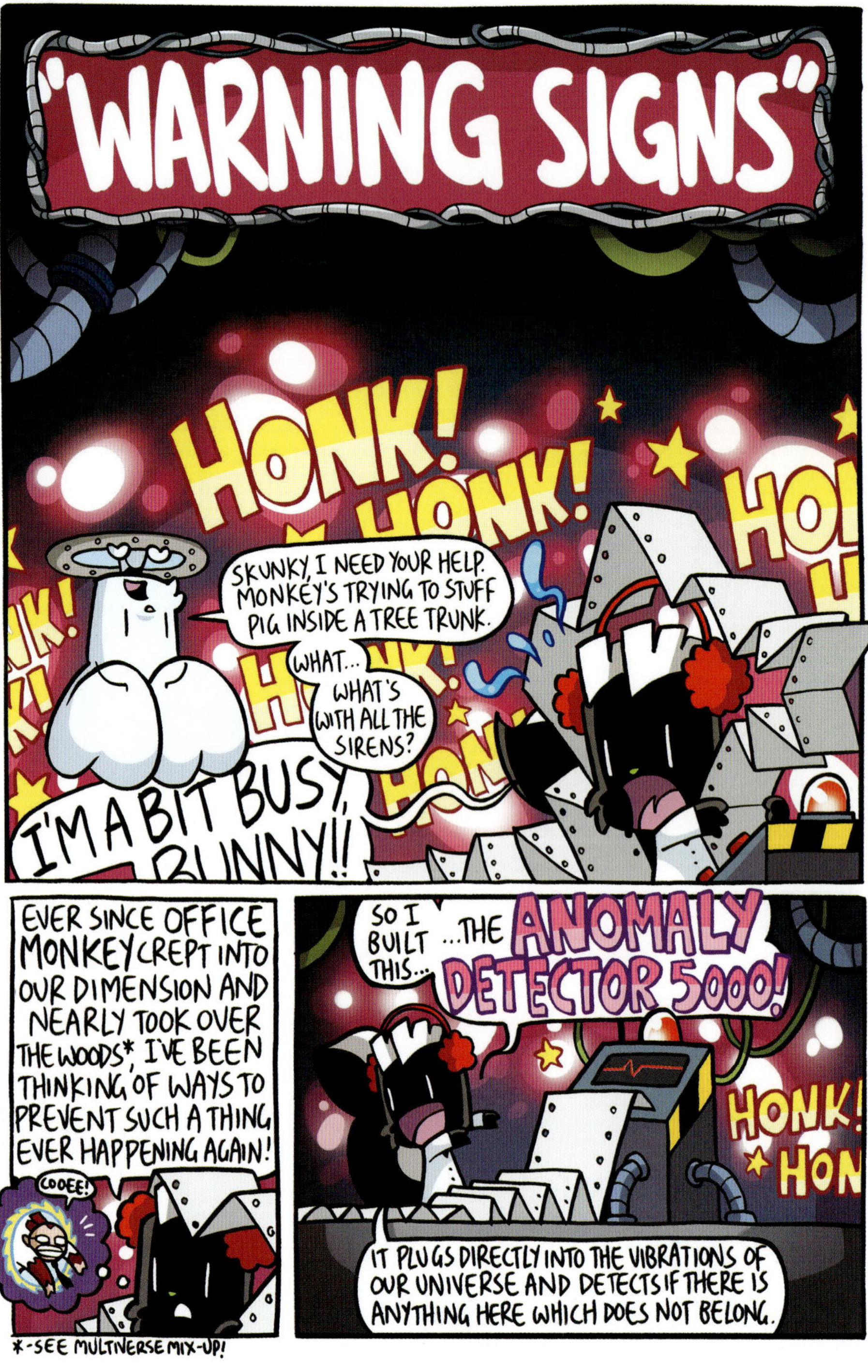
"WARNING SIGNS"
HONK!
HONK!
SKUNKY, I NEED YOUR HELP. MONKEY'S TRYING TO STUFF PIG INSIDE A TREE TRUNK.
WHAT... WHAT'S WITH ALL THE SIRENS?
I'M A BIT BUSY, BUNNY!!
EVER SINCE OFFICE MONKEY CREPT INTO OUR DIMENSION AND NEARLY TOOK OVER THE WOODS*, I'VE BEEN THINKING OF WAYS TO PREVENT SUCH A THING EVER HAPPENING AGAIN!
COOEE!
SO I BUILT THIS...
...THE ANOMALY DETECTOR 5000!
HONK!
IT PLUGS DIRECTLY INTO THE VIBRATIONS OF OUR UNIVERSE AND DETECTS IF THERE IS ANYTHING HERE WHICH DOES NOT BELONG.

*-SEE MULTIVERSE MIX-UP!

ONLY PROBLEM IS...
...I THINK IT'S MALFUNCTIONING!!
SMASH! SMASH!
IT WON'T SHUT UP!
AH.
THAT'S BETTER.
BEEWOO
I'VE ALSO BEEN TAKING OTHER MEASURES. I DOWNSIZED THE RESET BUTTON WHICH DEFEATED OFFICE MONKEY...INTO THIS STYLISH PORTABLE VERSION!
(I ALSO MADE AN ANTI-RESET BUTTON, FOR WHEN IT ALL INVARIABLY GOES WRONG).
OUR BEST DEFENCE, HOWEVER, AGAINST ANYTHING UNTOWARD ENTERING INTO OUR WORLD...

...IS THIS, THE ALL-SEEING EYE!
I'VE SPENT MONTHS HIDING CAMERAS...
...IN THE TREES...
...THE HEDGES...
...DOWN TOILETS...
...UP IN THE SKY...
NOW I CAN OBSERVE EVERY INCH OF THE WOODS!
I CAN TRACK ANY ANOMALY AS SOON AS IT APPEARS!
ISN'T THAT A BIT INVASIVE... ...OOH! THERE'S MONKEY!

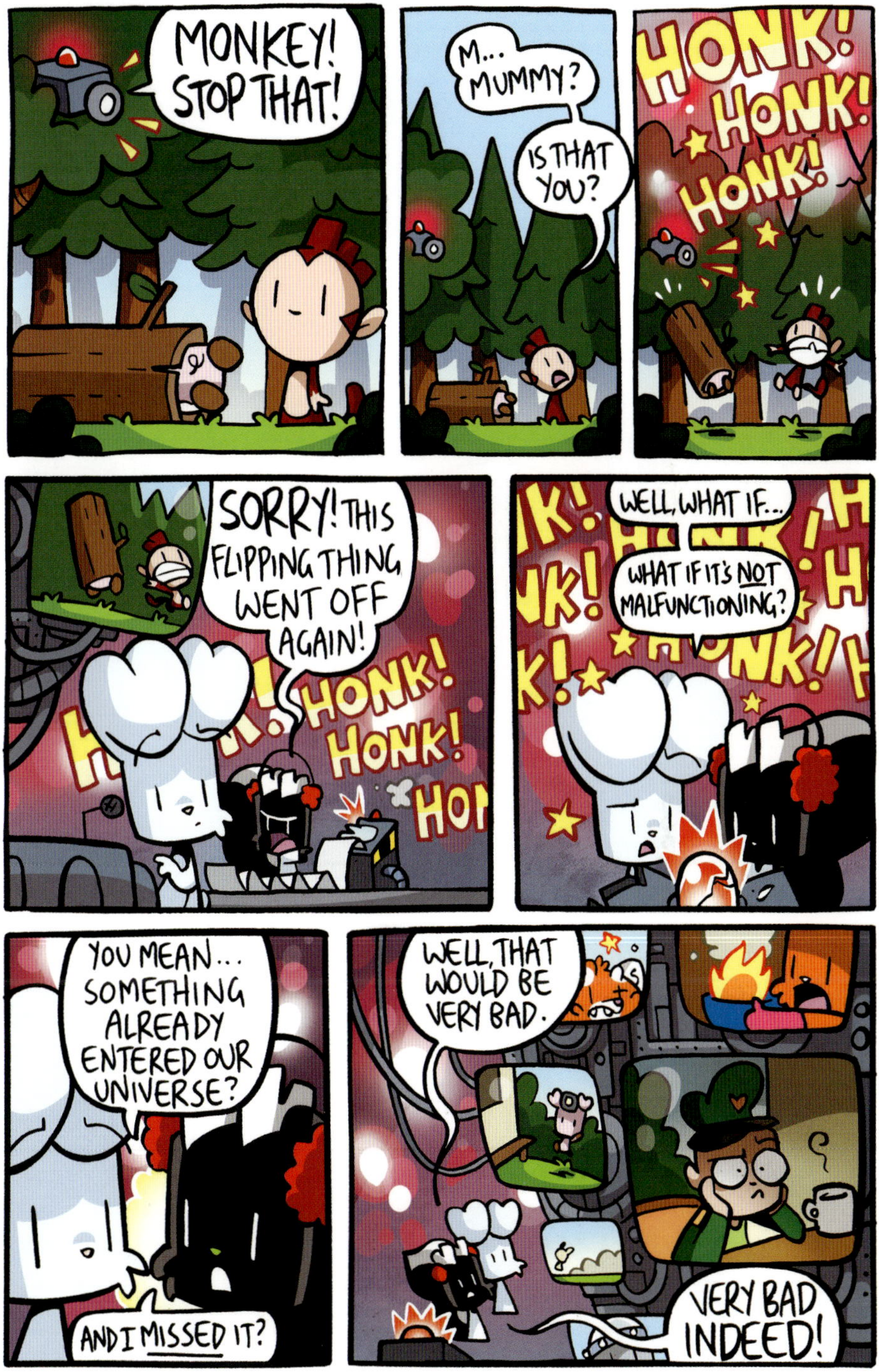
MONKEY! STOP THAT!
M... MUMMY?
IS THAT YOU?
HONK! HONK! HONK!
SORRY! THIS FLIPPING THING WENT OFF AGAIN!
HONK! HONK! HON
WELL, WHAT IF...
WHAT IF IT'S NOT MALFUNCTIONING?
YOU MEAN... SOMETHING ALREADY ENTERED OUR UNIVERSE?
AND I MISSED IT?
WELL, THAT WOULD BE VERY BAD.
VERY BAD INDEED!

"BISCUITS"
SIGH...
THE WEIRD WOODS WALL
PARK WARDEN
ALL THESE STRANGE, BIZARRE EVENTS HAPPENING IN THE WORLD OF BUNNY -VS- MONKEY...
AND YET...
...I STILL CAN'T FIND WHAT'S CAUSING THE GLITCH!
SLAM!
BLAGH!
AGH!

BIP
BIP
BIP
YOU'RE NOT BISCUITS.
I...
I'M NOT?
BANANAS! NOT BISCUITS!
BANANISCUITS!
WAIT, MONKEY IS A SCIENTIST NOW?
WELL, SINCE SKUNKY'S BEEN BUSY WATCHING HIS TV SHOWS...
I THOUGHT I'D GIVE IT A GO!
SO I TAPED A SAT-NAV TO PIG'S HEAD, AND BLUETOOTHED IT TO THESE VOICE CONTROLS!
BIP
BIP
NEEDS A LITTLE... FINE-TUNING THOUGH!
STOMP!
STOMP!
STOMP!

BIP BIP BIP BIP!
UNDER-PANTS!
UNDERPANTS, THIS WAY!
BIP BIP BIP BIP BIP BIP BI
BANANAS, PIG! BANANAAAS!
UNDERPAAAAAANTS!
I'M PRETTY GOOD AT SCIENCE. MAYBE I COULD RECONFIGURE THIS THING AND GET PIG LOOKING FOR...
UNDERPANTS!
NOW LOOK, I CAN EXPLAIN.
PIG, I'M LOOKING FOR A GLITCH, SOMETHING ...NOT QUITE RIGHT IN YOUR SURROUNDINGS.
CAN YOU...
CAN YOU FIND IT FOR ME?

GARDEN FURNITURE!!
BIP BIP BIP
OHHH NO YOU DON'T, I FOUND THIS, IT'S MINE!
NO, PIG. THE GLITCH! FIND THE GLITCH.
BIP BIP BIP
BALLOON!!
NO, THE GLITCH.
A CHEESE HAT!
YES?
NO, THE GLITCH!!
TURN LEFT AT THE HEDGE...
TRAVEL STRAIGHT FOR TWO MILES...
BIP BIP!
YOU HAVE REACHED YOUR DESTINATION.
WEENIE? WEENIE CAUSES THE GLITCH?
NO, SILLY!
WEENIE HAS BISCUITS!
I WANTED BANANAS.
WELL, I SUPPOSE THIS WILL DO FOR NOW.

"MAGIC BUNNY"
BRMMMMMMM!
MORNING, BUNNY!
LOVELY DAY, ISN'T IT?
LOVELY DAY TO BE RIDING THE...
PRIZE FLOWERS
MONKEY! YOU MONSTER!
...LAWNMOWER 5000!!
MY BELOVED FLOPPEDY BLOSSOMS, ...DESTROYED!
UNLESS...

PLOMP
THERE! I CAN JUST MAGIC THE WHOLE FLOWER BED BACK TO LIFE!
PLOMP! PLOMP! PLOMP!
HMM. HOW IS ZIS DONE? CGI?
I ALREADY TOLD YOU, LE FOX. EVER SINCE I BECAME ONE WITH THE MOLECULAR STREAM, I'VE HAD THIS STRONG CONNECTION TO NATURE!
I CAN MAKE ANYTHING GROW JUST BY WISHING IT!!
YOU HAVEN'T TOLD ME ZIS.
DID I NOT? I THOUGHT WE'D HAD THIS CONVERSATION BEFORE.

YOU? A MAGIC BUNNY?! I DON'T BELIEVE IT!
I AM, SO YOU'D BETTER WATCH OUT!
OH YEAH? WHY? WHAT ARE YOU GONNA DO?
THIS.
DINK!
FLOOMP
AND YOUR SILLY MOWER, TOO. MAYBE NOW YOU'LL STAY OUT OF TROUBLE.
FLOOMP
NOPE.
QUITE THE OPPOSITE.

LA LA LA.
OH! WHAT A LOVELY FLOWER!
THANKS! IT'S GROWING OUT OF MY NOSE!
EEK!
WHERE ARE YOU GOING? I WANT TO SHOW YOU THE BEAUTY OF NATURE!
BRMMM
I AM AT ONE WITH MY SURROUNDINGS!
BRMMM
THE WORLD IS FILLED WITH MAGIC!

BRMMM
OOPS.
PRIZE FLOWERS 2.0
RIGHT! YOU'RE REALLY GOING TO PAY THIS TIME...
AHEM.
ALLOW ME.
THAT'S ENOUGH! YOU'VE SHAVED ALL THE NATURE OFF ME!
BZZZ
NON NON.
JUST A BIT MORE OFF ZE BUTT.

"PAUSE!"
SIGH!
LOOK, I'LL EXPLAIN IT AGAIN. I'M GOING TO PRESS THIS BUTTON, WHICH WILL ACTIVATE THAT HASTILY CONSTRUCTED EJECTOR SEAT, PROPELLING YOU HIGH INTO THE SKY WITH ONLY A PAIR OF BARELY ADEQUATE WINGS TO CARRY YOU. MY PLAN IS FOR YOU TO CRASH-LAND FACE-FIRST ON THE OTHER SIDE OF THE RAVINE - I CAN'T REMEMBER WHY - BUT IF YOU DON'T MAKE IT, THEN THAT'S FINE TOO.
ANY QUESTIONS?
SNRF?
SORRY, CAN'T HEAR YOU. I'M EATING CHIPS.
BOOP!
P-DOING

HNNNGG
BLPP!
GNARF!
YEARGH!
BLPP!
DONK!
THE GLITCH!! IT'S HAPPENING AGAIN!
ALICE! CAN YOU HEAR ME? ENACT PROTOCOL 556 IMMEDIATELY!

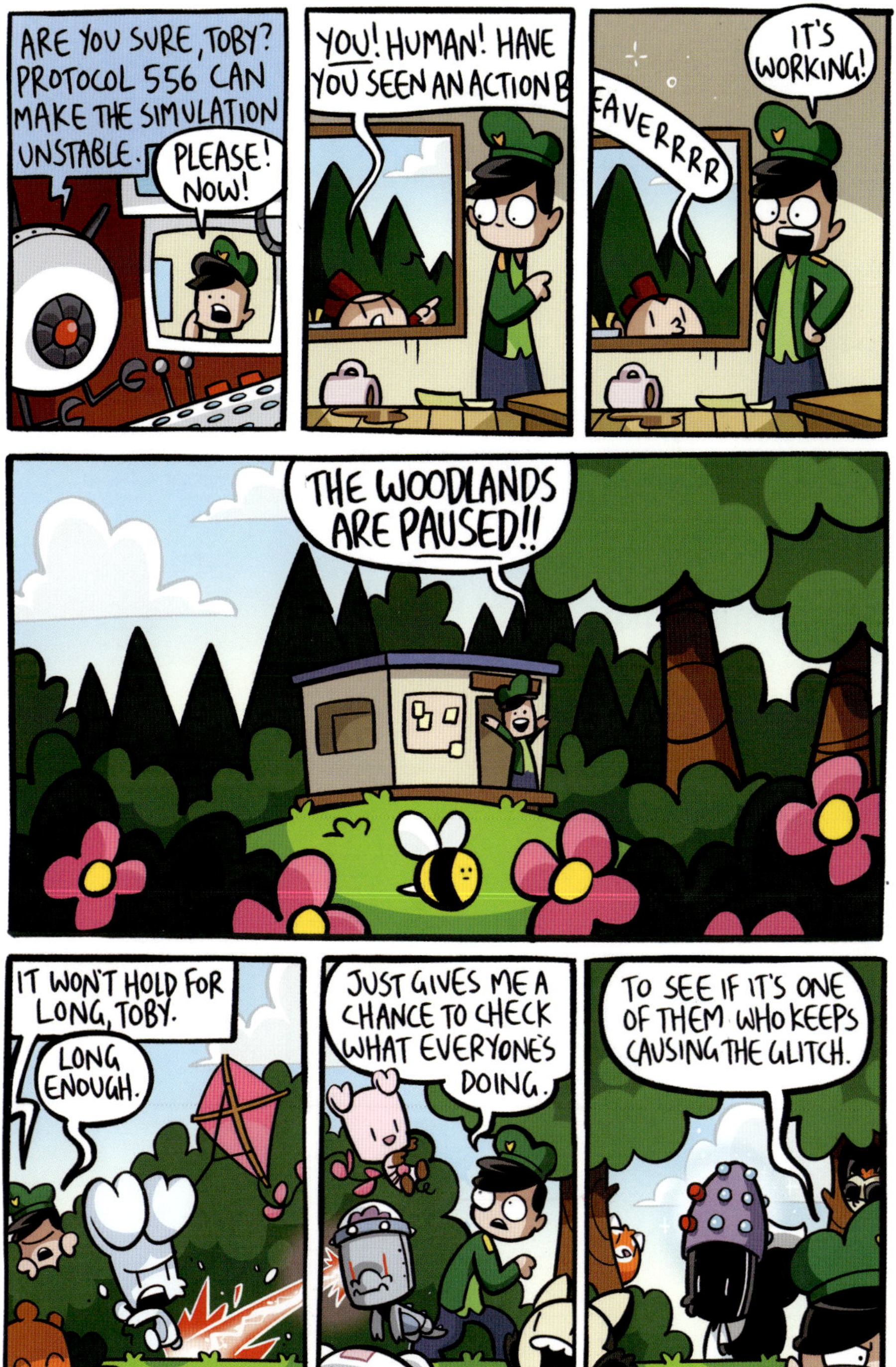
ARE YOU SURE, TOBY? PROTOCOL 556 CAN MAKE THE SIMULATION UNSTABLE.
PLEASE! NOW!
YOU! HUMAN! HAVE YOU SEEN AN ACTION B
EAVERRRR
IT'S WORKING!
THE WOODLANDS ARE PAUSED!!
IT WON'T HOLD FOR LONG, TOBY.
LONG ENOUGH.
JUST GIVES ME A CHANCE TO CHECK WHAT EVERYONE'S DOING.
TO SEE IF IT'S ONE OF THEM WHO KEEPS CAUSING THE GLITCH.

HANG ON.
MAYBE THIS THING ON SKUNKY'S HEAD CAUSED THE GLITCH.
WHATEVER IT IS.
IT'S A LOCALISED E.M.P. FORCEFIELD.
WHU-
ALICE, I SAID PAUSE THE SIMULATION!
ALICE CAN'T HEAR YOU. THIS HELMET BLOCKS OUT ALL EXTERNAL SIGNALS.
LEAVING ME FREE OF YOUR CONTROL, SO I CAN FIND OUT WHAT YOU'RE DOING!
AUGH!
GET BACK HERE!
MUNCH
OH, SORRY.
I'M MEANT TO BE PAUSED.
I FORGOT.

"DEJA VU"
ALICE! ALICE, CAN YOU HEAR ME?!
NYAHAHAHAA!!
SKUNKY? WH... WHAT'S GOING ON?
OW.
BZZZZZZ

THIS GUY, THE HOO-MAN, THE PARK WARDEN, HE'S THE ANOMALY I'VE BEEN LOOKING FOR. HE DOESN'T BELONG HERE!
TOBY!
I LOST YOU!
ALICE! THE ANIMALS HAVE TURNED ON ME!
I GOT SO CLOSE.
SO CLOSE.
PULL ME OUT!
RESET THE YEAR!
RESET THE WHAT?

RESET.
THE.
YEAR.
BOOM
THESE FEELINGS.
THIS DÉJÀ VU.

THESE MEMORIES.
THEY'RE NOT IMAGINARY.
THE WORLD HAS BEEN RESETTING.
AND OVER.
OVER.
AND OVER AND OVER AND OVER AND...
I'M SORRY EVERYONE, I PROMISE T
NOOOO
BUNNY VS MONKEY
AHH, I...
I THINK WE'LL BE THE JUDGE OF THAT.
BOOP!
WHAT?

THE PORTABLE ANTI-RESET BUTTON!! STOPS YOU FROM REBOOTING US ALL.
SO NOW YOU'RE STUCK HERE.
WITH THE REST OF US.
AND YOU'RE GOING TO TELL US **EXACTLY** WHAT'S GOING ON.

"THE STORY SO FAR"
OKAY! OKAY! I'LL TELL YOU EVERYTHING!
JUST DON'T LET MONKEY GUNGE ME!
AW.
BUT I HAVE LOADS.
IT ALL STARTED MANY YEARS AGO, WITH AN EXTRAORDINARILY SECRET ORGANISATION WHO HID THEIR LABORATORY IN THE WOODS...
GASP! MEANIECORP! I REMEMBER THEM!

MEANIECORP CONDUCTED THE MOST EXTREME AND BIZARRE SCIENTIFIC EXPERIMENTS IMAGINABLE.
I DIDN'T KNOW THIS WHEN I JOINED. I WAS A TRAINEE, A FRESH-FACED COMPUTER SCIENCES GRADUATE, TASKED WITH WHAT SEEMED LIKE A PRETTY BENIGN PROJECT.
H... HELLO?
I WAS HIRED TO CREATE A COMPUTER PROGRAM!!
OOOOOOH.
IT WASN'T AS FUN AS IT SOUNDS. MEANIECORP WANTED ME TO INVENT NEW TEXT-BASED SOFTWARE RUNNING RANDOMLY GENERATED CONFLICTS.
OOOOOOH.

BASICALLY ONE VARIABLE, WHICH THEY HAD ME CALL B, WAS TO DISRUPT THE CODE OF AN OPPOSING VARIABLE, WHICH THEY CALLED M, AND VICE VERSA.
>90-//M INS.
>RUN B WHEN ^75
>B WINS
ONCE ONE WAS DEFEATED, THE PROGRAM WOULD RESET, AND THEN RUN AGAIN. SOMETIMES THE OUTCOME WOULD BE DIFFERENT, SOMETIMES IT WOULD BE THE SAME.
>0//12 M
>CANCEL B
>M WINS
MY BRAIN FEELS SLEEPY.
THAT'S EXACTLY HOW I FELT. MY WORK WAS BORING.
SO, TO KEEP MYSELF AMUSED, I TRIED TO GIVE THE PROGRAM A LITTLE MORE...
...CHARACTER.
THAT WAS MY FIRST MISTAKE.
I CHANGED 'B' INTO THE WORD 'BUNNY'...
>LET BUNNY//RUN
>BUNNY NEXT 10
>FOR 10 = "23"
>THEN GO TO: MON
>MONKEY WINS
AND 'M' INTO THE WORD 'MONKEY'.
WHAT?
WHAT?

I ASSIGNED BASIC ICONS TO EACH, SO IT WOULD BE MORE FUN TO WATCH THEM DEFEAT EACH OTHER.
>RUN WHEN
>PRINT //
> WINS
THEN I GOT A BIT ...CARRIED AWAY.
I INTRODUCED MORE VARIABLES INTO THEIR CONFLICTS.
>WHEN + =
> GO TO
>+2 // RUN 7
> WINS
WITH ICONS FOR EACH.
SOON, I SWITCHED TO FULL-SCREEN VISUALS. THE GRAPHICS WERE VERY BASIC AT FIRST...
BUNNY + HOSE
MONKEY + SANDWICH
...BUT THE CODE RUNNING BEHIND IT WAS BECOMING INCREASINGLY COMPLEX.
BUNNY WINS!
THE OTHER MEANIECORP SCIENTISTS NOTICED WHAT I HAD BEEN DOING, AND GATHERED AROUND TO WATCH EACH FIGHT.
THERE WAS ONE SCIENTIST IN PARTICULAR.
HER NAME WAS ALICE.
BLURGH! GROSS!
TELL US MORE ABOUT ME HITTING BUNNY!
OKAY! OKAY!

OVER TIME, THE GRAPHICS STARTED IMPROVING. I INTRODUCED NEW CHARACTERS, NEW LOCATIONS. THE CONFLICTS WERE STILL RANDOM, BUT NOW THEY WERE STRETCHING OUT INTO LONGER AND LONGER STORYLINES...
CLONK!
FRPP!
OOOOW
OOOSH!
THIS GAME SOUNDS FUN!
CAN WE PLAY IT?
YOU ARE IT.
THIS IS THE GAME.

I CREATED YOU ALL INSIDE A COMPUTER. YOU'RE PIECES OF CODE RUNNING AROUND AN EVER-EXPANDING SIMULATION!
I CALLED IT!
AND YOU'D NEVER HAVE KNOWN, I WOULDN'T EVEN BE HERE, IF IT WASN'T FOR THE GLITCH.
YOU SEE, I STARTED ADDING REAL-WORLD LOCATIONS INTO THE SIMULATION, INCLUDING MEANIECORP ITSELF...
EVENTUALLY, ONE OF THE STORYLINES LED MONKEY TO UNLEASH A 'MOSHOGGOTH' FROM UNDERNEATH IT...
...WHICH ULTIMATELY CAUSED MEANIECORP TO VANISH.
ONCE GONE, ITS CODE ERASED ITSELF FROM THE SIMULATION.

ALICE AND I HAD POPPED OUT FOR LUNCH WHILE THAT PARTICULAR STORYLINE WAS RUNNING.
ONLY TO DISCOVER, UPON OUR RETURN, THAT THE REAL-LIFE MEANIECORP HAD DISAPPEARED TOO!
SOOO... WHAT?
SOMETHING HAD GONE CATASTROPHICALLY WRONG! A GLITCH IN THE CODE HAD CAUSED AN EVENT INSIDE THE SIMULATION TO ECHO INTO THE REAL WORLD!!
WELL, THAT WOULD BE EXTREMELY DANGEROUS!
OF COURSE IT WOULD!
LIKE MATTER AND ANTIMATTER COLLIDING, IT COULD DE-STABILISE EVERYTHING!!
I KNOW!
LUCKILY, ALICE AND I HAD DEVELOPED A REMOTE VERSION OF THE SIMULATION, WHICH WE SET UP IN MY APARTMENT.

WE WORKED TOGETHER FOR YEARS, WATCHING EACH NEW STORYLINE UNFOLD. LOOKING FOR ANOTHER SIGN OF THE GLITCH.
THEN IT HAPPENED.
THE SIMULATION NOTICED US!
OOH! THAT'S UNUSUAL...
THE GLITCH, IT WAS CHANGING!
IT'S ESCALATING!!
WITH NO TIME TO LOSE, I WENT ON THE OFFENSIVE. I INSERTED MYSELF AS AN AVATAR INTO THE SIMULATION...
FZZZ
ALICE THEN REPLAYED PREVIOUS BUNNY VS MONKEY STORYLINES SO I COULD SNEAK AROUND INSIDE THEM, PLAYING INNOCENT, WATCHING FOR ANY SIGNS OF WHAT COULD BE CAUSING THE GLITCH.

MY RELATIONSHIP SUFFERED.
LA LA LA
WHEN I FINALLY NOTICED, I BUILT MYSELF ANOTHER ALICE.
FZZT.
HELLO, TOBY.
WITH ALICE 2.0'S IMMENSE CALCULATING POWER, WE BUILT OTHER SIMULATIONS. RAN COUNTLESS OTHER STORYLINES.
BUT WE ALWAYS CAME BACK TO BUNNY VS MONKEY.
THE GLITCH WAS ONLY IN THERE.
BOOM
SO WHEN IT HAPPENED LIVE, RIGHT BEFORE MY EYES...
... I KNEW WE HAD TO ACT!

ALICE RESTARTED THE YEAR, PUT EVERYTHING IN THE BUNNY VS MONKEY SIMULATION RIGHT BACK TO JANUARY.
EVENTS WOULD RANDOMISE OFF INTO DIFFERENT STORYLINES, BUT I FELT SURE THE GLITCH WOULD REPEAT...
A FEW WEEKS IN ...IT **DID!**
SO WE RESTARTED THE YEAR AGAIN.
AND AGAIN.
AND AGAIN.
NARROWING THE GLITCH INTO A CORNER.
THIS WAS MY **DÉJÀ VU!**
WE HAVE ALREADY LIVED THIS YEAR MANY TIMES!
FIVE HUNDRED AND NINETY EIGHT.
SO FAR.
WHAT!
EACH TIME I GET CLOSER TO FINDING THE BROKEN PIECE OF CODE IN YOUR WORLD, TO FINDING WHAT CAUSES THE **GLITCH!**

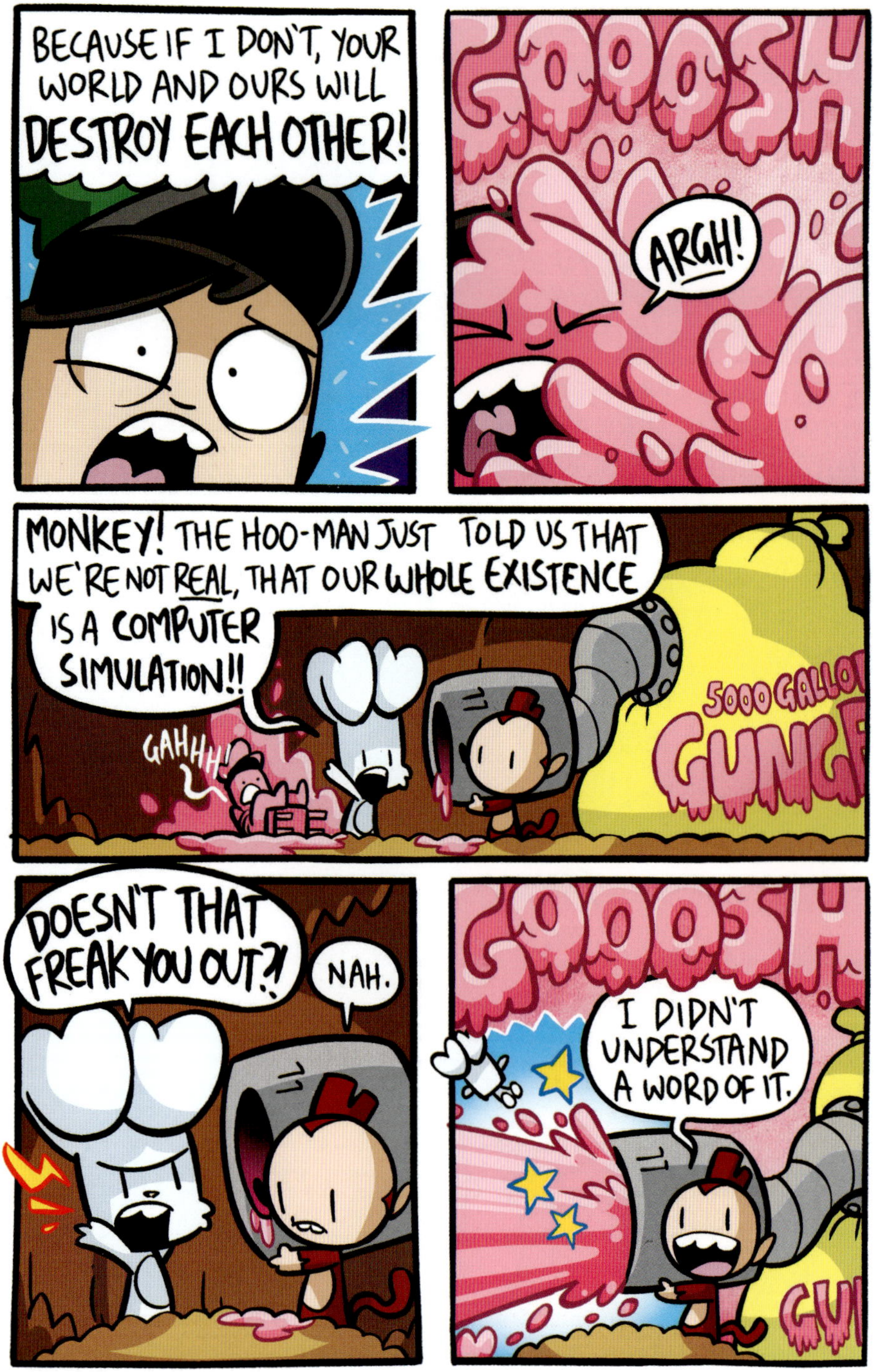
BECAUSE IF I DON'T, YOUR WORLD AND OURS WILL DESTROY EACH OTHER!
GOOOSH
ARGH!
MONKEY! THE HOO-MAN JUST TOLD US THAT WE'RE NOT REAL, THAT OUR WHOLE EXISTENCE IS A COMPUTER SIMULATION!!
GAHHH!
DOESN'T THAT FREAK YOU OUT?!
NAH.
GOOOSH
I DIDN'T UNDERSTAND A WORD OF IT.

"AN ESCAPE"
SO THAT'S IT, THEN.
WE'RE ALL JUST CHARACTERS INSIDE A COMPUTER SIMULATION.
EVERYTHING WE THOUGHT TO BE REAL... IS JUST AN ILLUSION!
I DON'T EXIST.
NONE OF US EXIST.
NOTHING MEANS ANYTHING ANY MORE.
ARE YOU KIDDING? THIS IS GREAT NEWS!

FOR ONE, IT FINALLY ANSWERS THE BIGGEST QUESTION IN THE WHOLE UNIVERSE: THE SECRET OF EXISTENCE! WE ARE IMAGINED, CREATED TO PLAY OUT OUR LIVES FOR THE VIEWING PLEASURE OF A MORE INTELLIGENT SPECIES!!
HELLO.
FOR TWO, IF ALL WE ARE IS CHARACTERS IN A SIMULATION, THEN OUR ACTIONS HAVE NO MORAL CONSEQUENCE. WE ARE FREE! FREE TO DO WHATEVER WE WANT!!

FOR EXAMPLE...MONKEY? I'VE ALWAYS DESPISED WORKING FOR YOU. YOU'RE AN IDIOT WITH A BUM FOR A FACE.
B...B...
YOU SEE? WE'RE FREE! FREE OF OUR SOCIAL OBLIGATIONS!!
WHEEEE!
LE SIGH.
CAN YOU ALL STOP HAVING MEETINGS IN MY SECRET TUNNELS, PLEASE?
FLUSH!
LE FOX, DID YOU HEAR THE NEWS?
I HEARD. AND I DO NOT BELIEVE IT.
ZIS HUMAN MUST BE LYING.
I AM VERY REAL.
GULP

HOW ELSE COULD I BE FEELING SUCH AN EXCITEMENT ABOUT BOPPING HIM ON ZE HEAD WITH MY LUNCH?
HEE HEE OOF!!
GNARGH!
BOMP!
ALICE! QUICKLY! THE HELMET'S OFF!
I'M ON IT, TOBY!
FOR WHAT IT'S WORTH EVERYONE, I'M VERY SORRY.
FZZ!
BPP BOOP!
NO! NOOOO!!

SKUNKY, HE'S GOING TO GO HOME AND RESET THE YEAR AGAIN!
WE'LL FORGET EVERYTHING HE'S TOLD US!
BUNNY, I MAY BE NEWLY CAREFREE, BUT I'M NOT STUPID.
I PUT A TRACKER ON HIM.
MONKEY? WOULD YOU CARE TO REVEAL THE NEXT STAGE OF MY PLAN?
I DON'T HAVE A BUM FOR A FACE.
SAT-NAV PIG!
BIP!
BIP! BIP!
OOH!
IS IT BISCUITS?

'LAND OF THE HOO-MANS'
IT'S THIS WAY!
BIP BIP BIP
YOU MEAN...
...WE HAVE TO LEAVE THE WOODS?
TO VENTURE INTO THE LAND OF HOO-MANS!!
I PACKED A BLOW TORCH.
I PACKED LEMON PUFFS.

IT'S NOISIER THAN I CALCULATED.
IT'S SMELLIER THAN I CALCULATED.
BRUMM!
HONNKK
ROYDON 5m
NGTON 10m

I'VE BEEN TO THEIR CITY ONCE BEFORE.
OR AT LEAST, I THOUGHT I HAD.
BIP
BIP
HEDGEHOG TUNNEL
WAIT, DID A HEDGEHOG BUILD THIS TUNNEL?
THIS WAY!
BIP
BIP
I'M NOT SURE HE'S RIGHT.
PIG, ARE YOU UPSIDE DOWN?
THE HOO-MANS KEEP LOOKING AT ME FUNNY.
IT'S OKAY, THEY'RE NOT REAL.

THIS ONE SOUNDS REAL.
OW!
DONK!
IF WHAT THE WARDEN SAID WAS CORRECT, THIS IS ALL A SIMULATION.
CLAKKITY-CLACK
WAIT, BUT THE WARDEN LEFT THE SIMULATION.
SO HOW ARE WE STILL TRACKING HIM?
I HAVE NO IDEA.
WELCOME
HE'S IN THERE!
BOOF!
GRUNT
...BUT I AM VERY EXCITED TO FIND OUT.
BWOO

TOBY, THIS IS A VERY BAD IDEA.
IT'S THE ONLY WAY, ALICE! I HAVE TO UNPLUG THE SIMULATION!
I HAVE TO SHUT 'BUNNY VS MONKEY' DOWN FOR GOOD!
TOILETS.
BIG WOBBLY BOTTOM.
BZZT.
A... ALICE?
ARE YOU OKAY?
I DO APOLOGISE, TOBY. SOMEONE APPEARS TO HAVE WEDGED A LEMON PUFF INTO MY CIRCUITRY.
THAT...
THAT'S A GAG FROM YEAR ONE.
ALL RIGHT, HOO-MAN!! STEP AWAY FROM THE POWER CABLE!
SHRIEK! YOU CAN'T BE HERE, IN THE REAL WORLD, THAT'S NOT POSSIBLE!
UNLESS... THE GLITCH LET YOU IN.
GNAW GNAW!
IN WHICH CASE WE'RE TOO LATE.
THE FABRIC OF REALITY HAS BEEN STRETCHED SO WIDE...
...EXISTENCE ITSELF IS FALLING APART!
BUNNY VS MONKEY
GOOD.
NOW LET'S HAVE SOME FUN.

"STOLEN TECH"

HEE HEE HEE!
HEE HEE!
HEEE!
SKUNKY? WHY DID YOU TAKE ALL OF THE WARDEN'S COMPUTERS?
AHH, HE WON'T NEED THEM ANYMORE.
IT'S NOT POSSIBLE.
IT'S NOT POSSIBLE.

AND BESIDES, IF HE WAS RIGHT, AND IF THE WHOLE WORLD AS WE KNOW IT IS JUST A SIMULATION...
TAP TAP
...THEN ISN'T IT ABOUT TIME WE WERE THE ONES IN CHARGE OF IT?
BWOOOOOM!
THE ALL-SEEING EYE, YOU'VE CONNECTED HIS TECHNOLOGY TO YOUR OWN!
INDEED! AND NOW...

BOOP!
I CAN CONTROL ANYTHING IN THE WOODS!!
WEENIE, DO YOU HAVE ANY LEMON PUFFS LEFT?
SORRY, I STUFFED THEM ALL INTO THE ROBOT.
CRUMP!
GIANT LEMON PUFF!
IT WORKS!
LEMON PUFFS
MAX
GIVE ME A GO! I WANT TO DISRUPT REALITY TOO!!
JAB!
JAB!

THIS IS NOT COOL.
NOT COOL!!
SPLOOOSH!
YES!
MORE SHARKS!
MORE SHARKS!
UHH.
HANG ON.
SUDDENLY IT FEELS VERY DRAUGHTY IN HERE.
AHA!
FOUND IT!

THE CHARACTER CUSTOMISATION MODULE!
FZZP!
THIS IS WHAT THE WARDEN USED TO DESIGN US. HOW WE LOOK, HOW WE FEEL, ALL OUR ATTRIBUTES AND STATISTICS!
BLPP!
AND NOW...
...WE CAN CHANGE THEM!
BLPP!
A MONKEY SAUSAGE?!
YOU MEAN... THAT LITTLE BOX CAN REWRITE WHO WE ARE?
YES! YOU CAN BE ANYTHING!
BLPP!
NOT THIS.
NOT THIS!
UPGRADE YOURSELF. BECOME THE CHARACTER YOU ALWAYS THOUGHT YOU SHOULD BE.
THE ONLY QUESTION IS...
...WHO DO YOU WANT TO BE?

"UPGRADES"
AHH, WHAT A BEAUTIFUL DAY TO BE ME,
BUNNY, GUARDIAN OF THE WOODLANDS!
CHIRP!
CHIRP!
WHAT'S THAT, SONGBIRD? YOU WISH TO DELIGHT IN A DAZZLING DISPLAY OF NATURE?

THEN WITH MY WOODLAND POWERS, I SHALL MAKE IT SO!
STOP THAT.
AH! LE FOX! HOW LOVELY TO SEE YOU!
WHERE DID ZE BIG SILLY HAT COME FROM?
DONK!
I CREATED IT FROM THE ESSENCE OF GAIA HERSELF!
AND WHY ARE YOU TALKING SO WEIRD? BUNNY, WHAT IS GOING ON?
IT'S THIS, OKAY? THE CHARACTER CUSTOMISATION MODULE!!
SKUNKY SAID IT WOULD ALLOW ME TO BE WHOEVER I WANT TO BE.
WELL, SINCE I'VE BEEN BLESSED WITH THESE STRANGE POWERS...
I DON'T REMEMBER ZIS.
I THOUGHT, WHY NOT RAMP THEM UP A BIT?
INCREASE MY STATS TO MAX.

SO, I HAVE BECOME THE TRUE GUARDIAN OF THE WOODLANDS!!
I'D LIKE TO SEE MONKEY TRY TO TAKE OVER NOW!
SO WOULD I!
YOINK!
HAR HAR! THE MODULE IS MINE! I CAN TURN MYSELF INTO ANYTHING I WANT TO BE!
AND I WANT TO BE...
A HUGE PAIR OF PANTS! WHICH FIRES LASERS!
BLPPP!
NO, WAIT, A VAMPIRE MAGGOT!!
BLPPP!

ORRR, I COULD JUST UPGRADE MY MONKEY SKIN...
...INTO COLD, HARD METAL...
...AND
BLPPP!
METALMONKEY
IS BACK, BABY!
BRING IT ON, TIN CAN! I HAVE THE POWER OF THE WOODS ON MY SIDE!

AHEM!
ZIS...MODULE. IT CAN TURN YOU INTO WHATEVER YOU WANT TO BE?
YES.
BON. ZEN I WANT TO BE...
BLPP
OOF!
CLANG!
...SOMEWHERE ELSE.

"BEEFY SQUIRREL"
DING!
FULLY CHARGED!
NYAH HA! NOW I, METAL MONKEY, AM RUNNING AT 100% IT'S TIME TO CRUSH THESE WOODS UNDER AN IRON FIST!
WHAP!
BUH?
WHAP!
BUH BUH?

NOT TODAY, MONKEY! A VERY SPECIAL EVENT IS HAPPENING AND, AS THE GUARDIAN OF THE WOODLANDS, I'LL NOT LET YOU RUIN IT!
SPECIAL EVENT? LIKE WHAT?

WEENIE AND PIG ARE HAVING A PICNIC!
THAT'S NOT A SPECIAL EVENT! IT HAPPENS EVERY OTHER WEEK!
WELL, ANYWAY, I'M KEEPING THEM SAFE.
NOT FOR LONG, MOSS-FACE! I'M GOING TO TRAMPLE THEIR PANINIS!
RIIIP!
NOT IF I GROW A TREE IN YOUR WAY!
YOU MIGHT HAVE MAGIC POWERS, BUNNY, BUT I HAVE...
CRAACK!
...ROBOT STRENGTH!!

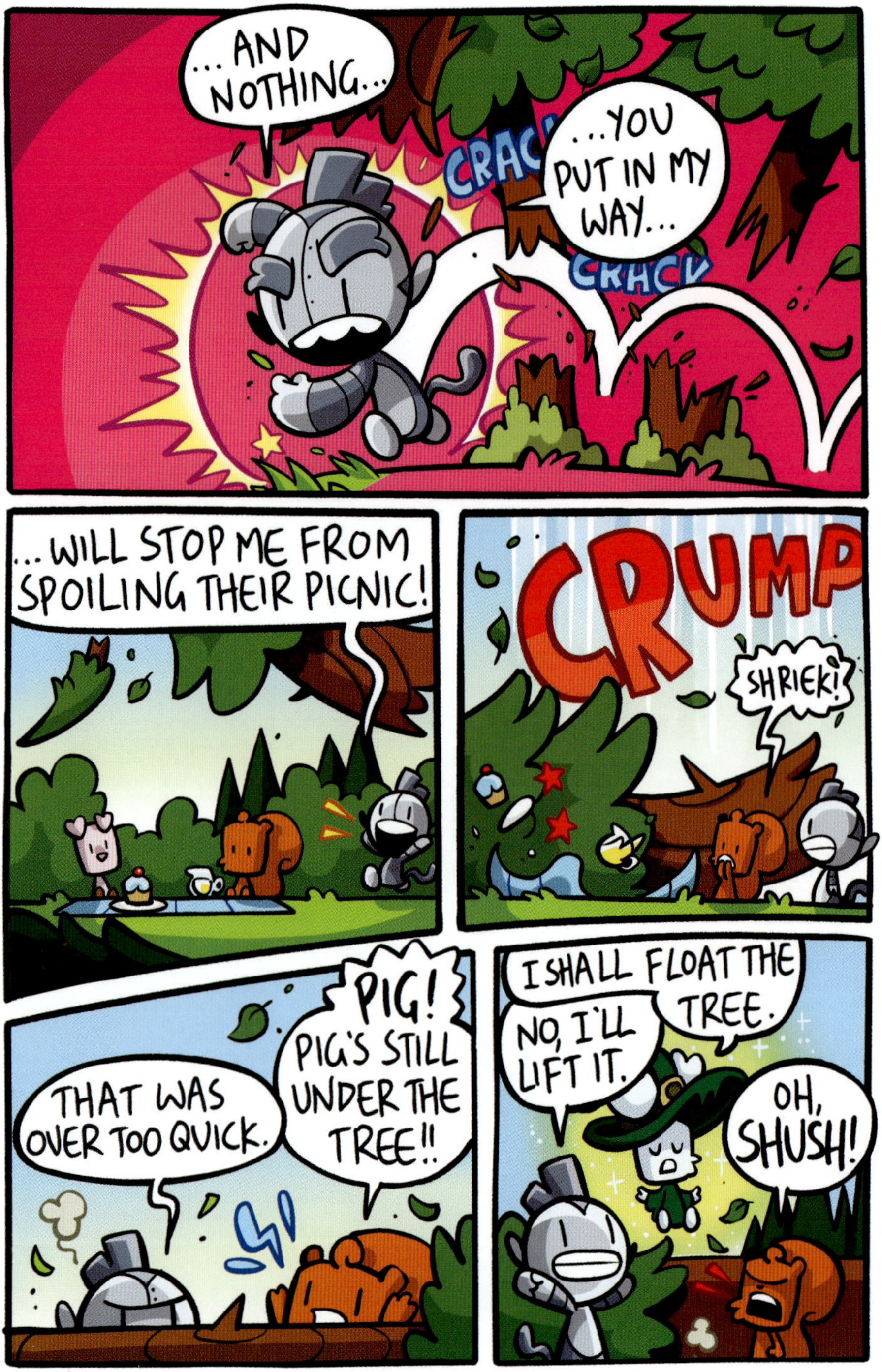

...AND NOTHING...
CRACK
...YOU PUT IN MY WAY...
CRACK
...WILL STOP ME FROM SPOILING THEIR PICNIC!
CRUMP
SHRIEK!
THAT WAS OVER TOO QUICK.
PIG! PIG'S STILL UNDER THE TREE!!
I SHALL FLOAT THE TREE.
NO, I'LL LIFT IT.
OH, SHUSH!

I HAVE THE MODULE, SO I'M GOING TO USE IT TO FIX YOUR MESS.
AND I'LL TURN MYSELF INTO WHAT I'VE ALWAYS WANTED TO BE.
BLPP!
IT'S WORKING!
IT'S WORKING!
BLPPP!
BLPPPP!
I'M BECOMING...
...AN ABSOLUTE POWER-HOUSE!!

HEY, LITTLE PIG, YOU OKAY UNDER THERE?
I CRUSHED MY MACARON.
HEAVE!
AND I...I THINK I'M SEEING THINGS.
OH, YOU'RE SEEING THE REAL WEENIE.
...AND FROM NOW ON, I'LL BE KEEPING US BOTH SAFE.
YAY!

"MODULE MADNESS"
STAND ASIDE, INNOCENTS! YOU'RE ABOUT TO BE PULVERISED BY THE COUNCIL OF DARK JUSTICE!
TINY STEVE!
BZZ!
METAL MONKEY!
MOOP!
ACTION COW!
YOU'VE BEEN USING THE MODULE THEN, HUH?
INDEED I HAVE.

I USED IT TO SHRINK METAL STEVE TO THE SIZE OF A BUTTERFLY!
BLPPPP!
SO HAPPY!
ACTION BEAVER WANTED TO BE A COW (NOT SURE WHY).
HONK!
I EVEN TRIED TO CHANGE SKUNKY, BUT HE SAID HE WAS ON THE TOILET.
I'M ON THE TOILET.
SEE?
BUT IT'S FINE, THE COUNCIL OF DARK JUSTICE WILL THRIVE WITHOUT HIM!
LET ME HAVE A LOOK AT THIS THING.
YOINK!
HOI!
WHIZZ
SO I COULD JUST TURN MYSELF INTO WHATEVER I WANT?
NO!
WELL, YES.
WELL, GIVE IT BACK!!
BZZP!
THAT'S IT, TINY STEVE! PROTECT THE MODULE!
YOINK!

HMM, MAYBE I DON'T NEED TO CHANGE. I'M ALREADY PRETTY GREAT.
WHIZZ!
THAT SAID...
...THERE'S ALWAYS SOME ROOM FOR IMPROVEMENT!
BLAT
NOW, LET'S SEE, WHAT BUTTON DO I PRESS TO GET X-RAY VISION?
CHOMP!
ACTION COW!

QUICK ESCAPE
FFFRRPP!
AGH!
EUGH!
GREAT JOB, ACTION COW! NOW BRING ME THE MODULE!
BRING...
ME...
I DON'T THINK HE'S COMING BACK.

STILL, WITHOUT ANY UPGRADES YOU'LL BE NO MATCH FOR MY ROBOT STRENGTH!
CLONK!
OH.
CRUMP!
MOOF!
ARGH!
YOU FOOL, ACTION COW! NOW AI WILL CHANGE HERSELF AND DEFEAT THE DARK COUNCIL!
OH, NOT ME.
BUH-KAWK!!
FAR MORE FUN TO UPGRADE ACTION COW INTO ACTION CHICKEN!
KEEP YOU QUIET FOR A BIT.
GMPHH!

"CODENAME P.I.G."
GROOOOOAARGHHH!
SPLAT!

RUN AWAY!!
IT'S A ...A...
WELL.
IT'S A...
CHOMP
UH OH.
HELP! IT'S GOT ME! I NEED HELP! I NEED...
YOU NEED A PIG.
I WAS GOING TO SAY BUNNY.
SECRET AGENT
CODENAME
P.I.G.
(PIG IS GREAT)
BREAKING COVER TO SAVE THE WORLD AGAIN!!

PIG! DID YOU USE THE MODULE?
I UPGRADED MY OWN CENTRAL INTELLIGENCE!
AND I INSTALLED A FEW EXTRA GADGETS TOO!
BEEBOOP AT YOUR SERVICE.
BEEBOOP, WE HAVE A CODE NINE. IDENTIFY!
ACCESSING SKUNKY'S DATABASE.
BEE BOOP!
BEE BOOP!
IT APPEARS TO BE ROBOTIC IN ORIGIN, SIR. PROTOTYPE #03. ONE OF SKUNKY'S FIRST-EVER INVENTIONS.
HMM. INTERESTING.
HWUH-PINGGG!
BURIED IN THE GROUND FOR YEARS...
...AND YET IT CHOOSES TO COME BACK NOW. BUT WHY?
BEEBOOP! FIRE UP JACKET BOOSTERS!
ARE YOU RETREATING, SIR?

NOPE.
I'M GOING IN.
SKK FFT FWOOM
GRUAW!
THUNK!

DOWNLOADING MAINFRAME CORE.
BRRP BPP BPP!
FILENAME: OBJECTIVES.
ICE CREAM?!
DING!
WHY, THE POOR THING'S JUST HUNGRY!
JUST SHARE YOUR ICE CREAM WITH IT, LUCKY!
BUT I DROPPED IT!!
THAT'S CASE CLOSED.
HELLO? DID YOU HEAR ME?
CASE CLOSED!

"YUM YUMS!"
MEANWHILE, QUITE DEEP UNDERGROUND.
IT'S 4 P.M.!
TIME FOR STRAWBERRY YUM-YUMS.
UM, WE RAN OUT OF STRAWBERRY YUM-YUMS, YOUR MAJESTY.
NONSENSE, WE HAVE A WHOLE ROOM FULL OF THEM.
WE DID, UNTIL YOU ATE THEM ALL.

YUM YUMS
HMM. I DON'T REMEMBER THAT.
IT WAS ONLY THIS MORNING.
THERE'S NOTHING ELSE FOR IT. WE MUST GO TO THE SURFACE AND GET SOME MORE!
GASP!
NO!
THE SURFACE?
YOUR MAJESTY, WE'RE THE UNDERCREATURES OF THE EARTH!
WE NEVER GO ABOVE GROUND!
WE DO WHEN WE NEED YUM-YUMS.
AND I HAVE A SUPPLIER IN THE WOODS.

CAN WE NOT INTEREST YOU IN SOMETHING ELSE FOR TEA?
A FRENCH HORN?
NOPE.
A VIENNESE FINGER!
A CHERRY DANISH?
NOPE.
NOPE.
A SPOTTED DICK!!
NOPE.
NOPE.
NOPE.
I MUST HAVE STRAWBERRY YUM-YUMS!
BUT...BUT, SIRE, THERE ARE ANIMALS IN THOSE WOODS...
EXIT
...AND THEY'RE A BIT...WEIRD.

NONSENSE, THEY'RE ALL PERFECTLY NORMAL ONCE YOU GET TO KNOW TH...
...EMMM.
CREEEAR!
FZZ
BOOM!
PRPPPPP!
BZ
FWOO
PRPPPPPPPPP!
KING AXOLOTL!
THE USUAL, IS IT?

HERE YOU GO. AND TRY TO MAKE THIS BATCH LAST, OKAY?
YUM-YUMS
SIRE?
SIRE, ARE YOU OKAY?
YUM-YUMS
WE ARE NEVER GOING TO THE SURFACE EVER AGAIN.
MM.
YUM-YUMS.

'FIGHT NIGHT'
AMONGST THE ROOTS HE SLEEPS..
BENEATH THE SLIPPERY WET MUD..
WAKING ONLY FOR TONIGHT...
...FOR TONIGHT IS HALLOWEEN, AND
THE BOGGOTH
...DEMANDS VENGEANCE!!
BOGGOTH!!
SCH
UUCK!

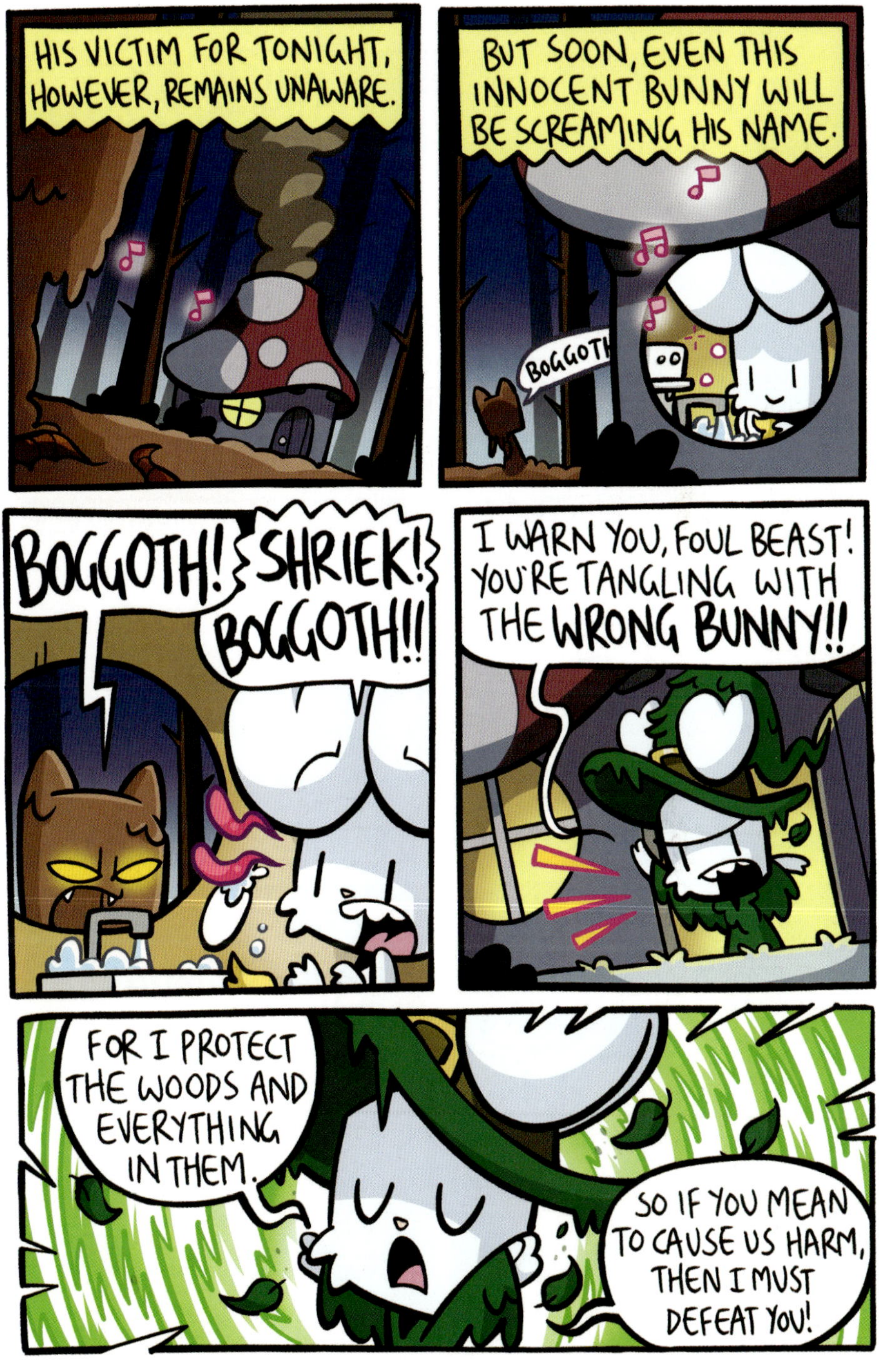
HIS VICTIM FOR TONIGHT, HOWEVER, REMAINS UNAWARE.
BUT SOON, EVEN THIS INNOCENT BUNNY WILL BE SCREAMING HIS NAME.
BOGGOTH
BOGGOTH!
SHRIEK! BOGGOTH!!
I WARN YOU, FOUL BEAST! YOU'RE TANGLING WITH THE WRONG BUNNY!!
FOR I PROTECT THE WOODS AND EVERYTHING IN THEM.
SO IF YOU MEAN TO CAUSE US HARM, THEN I MUST DEFEAT YOU!

OH.
HE'S GONE.
WHO'S GONE?
SHRIEK! BOGGOTH!
MONKEY! ARE YOU THE BOGGOTH?
NO, BUT HE SOUNDS AWESOME
DOES HE LIKE MUD ON A STICK? WILL THIS ATTRACT IT?
BOGGOTH!!
SHRIEK! BOGGOTH!
THE BOGGOTH!
THE BOGGOTH!
THE BOGGOTH!!
SLAM

WHAT DO WE DO NOW?
DO WE KEEP SAYING BOGGOTH?
CLUNK!
THE LIGHTS!
IT CUT THE POWER!
NO, WAIT. IT WAS ME. I WAS TRYING TO CHARGE UP MY BOTTOM.
Fzzp!
BOGGGGOTH!!
SHRIEK! BOGGOTH!!
RIGHT, THIS HAS GONE FAR ENOUGH.
SPLAT!

I DISPEL YOUR BODY BACK INTO THE GROUND, FOUL BOGGOTH! YOUR UNNATURAL FORM IS NOT WELCOME!!
BOGGOTH!
BOGGOTH! BOG OFF!
BOG OFF!
I WAS TELLING YOU BOTH TO BOG OFF!
LE FOX!
SHRIEK!
I FELL ASLEEP IN THE MUD, ALL RIGHT? I'M A FOX, SOMETIMES WE DO THAT.
HUH.
PANIC OVER!
NO BUT SERIOUSLY, BOG OFF.

"BUNNY VS MONKEY"
GRR! STUPID BUNNY, WITH HIS STUPID MAGICAL WOODLAND POWERS AND HIS STUPID FLOPPY STUPID LEAFY STUPID HAT!!
DOESN'T HE REALISE I AM METAL MONKEY, THE NEXT STAGE IN MONKEY EVOLUTION?!
I SHOULD BE RUNNING THESE WOODS...
...WITH MY SUPER-EXTENDABLE
ROBOTARMS!
PINCHY PINCHY

NYAH HA!
CLAMP! CLOMP!
WHO'S IN CHARGE NOW, BUNNY?! I GOT YOUR HOUSE!!
MONKEY, PUT THAT DOWN.
NO.
WHAT ARE YOU GOING TO DO, BUNNY? HIT ME WITH SOME FLOWERS? STICK A HEDGE UP MY NOSE?
OH, MONKEY.
I CAN DO FAR BETTER THAN THAT.

I COMMAND THE GROUND ITSELF TO DISAPPEAR FROM BENEATH YOUR FEET!!
NYAHH-HHH!!
RUMMMMBLE
THUNK!
GREAT! I'M STUCK! NOW WHAT?
NOW...
...WE PUT MY HOUSE BACK!!
OH, BOTTOMS.

CRUMP!
HA! COUGH! JOKE'S ON YOU, BUNNY! NOW YOU'RE STUCK WITH ME IN YOUR HOUSE FOREVER!
OH, IT WON'T BE SO BAD...
...AT LEAST NOW I HAVE SOMEWHERE TO CHARGE UP MY PHONE!!
GRRRGH!
BUNNY NEWS

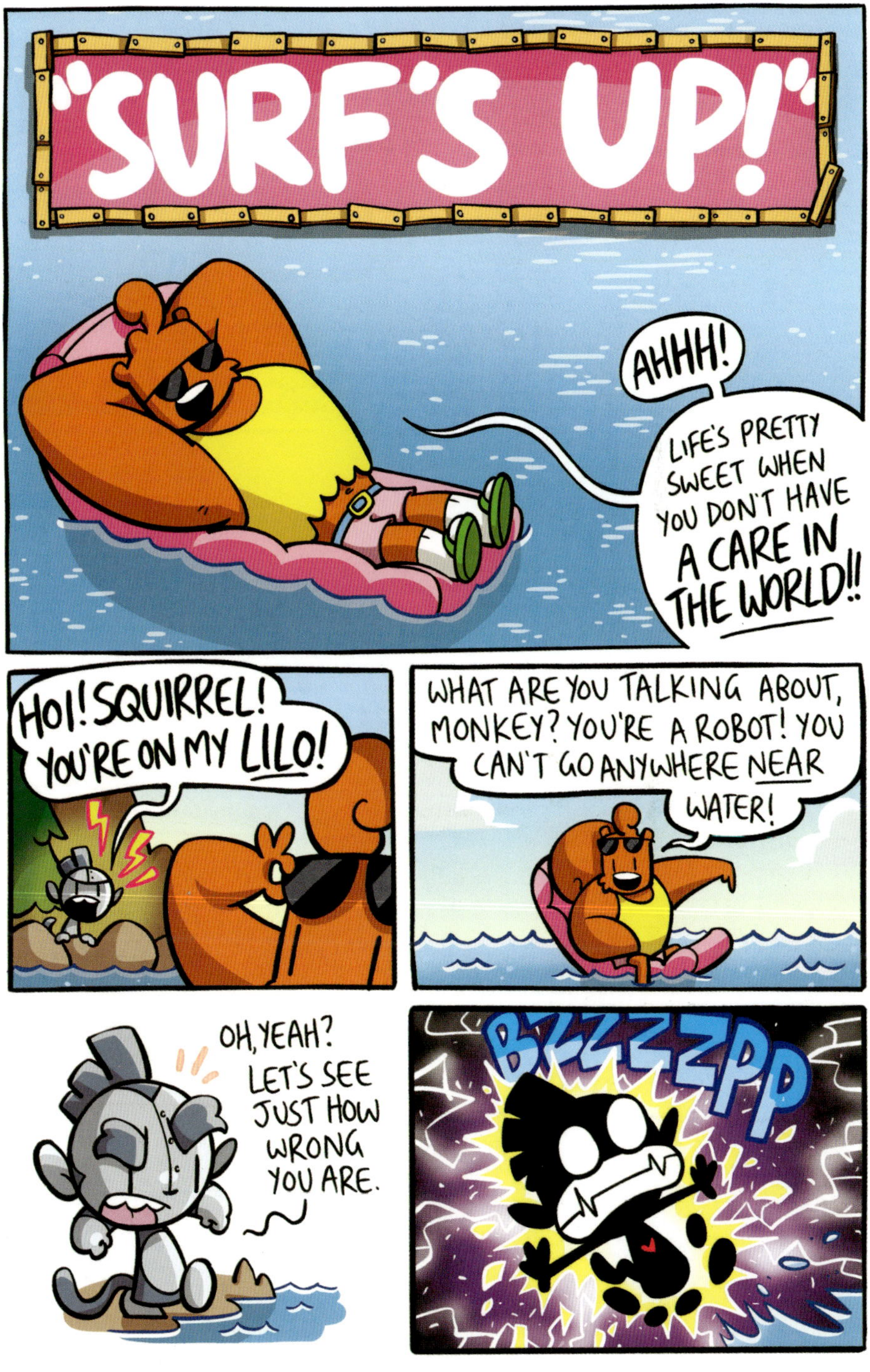
"SURF'S UP!"
AHHH!
LIFE'S PRETTY SWEET WHEN YOU DON'T HAVE A CARE IN THE WORLD!!
HOI! SQUIRREL! YOU'RE ON MY LILO!
WHAT ARE YOU TALKING ABOUT, MONKEY? YOU'RE A ROBOT! YOU CAN'T GO ANYWHERE NEAR WATER!
OH, YEAH?
LET'S SEE JUST HOW WRONG YOU ARE.
BZZZZPP

HA HA! SORRY, MONKEY, NO LILO FOR YOU! YOU CHOSE A RUBBISH UPGRADE!
BAH! EVER SINCE THAT SQUIRREL UPPED HER BRAVERY, SHE'S BEEN INTOLERABLE!
MAYBE IT'S TIME I SHOWED HER WHO'S REALLY IN CHARGE HERE!
HEY, WEENIE!
CANNON BALL!!
BZZZPP

OH, WELL DONE, MONKEY!! YOU JUST BURST THE LILO COMPLETELY!!
DOESN'T BOTHER ME! NOW I HAVE THE WHOLE LAKE TO MYSEL—
...NYOW!
...HMM, THIS IS NOT GOING TO WORK.
ACTIVATE SUCK MODE!!
HOOOOO!!

IF WATER'S THE PROBLEM...
URP!
UH OH.
MAYBE ALL THAT WATER ISN'T GOOD FOR MY INTERNAL CIRCUITS, EITHER!
BOILK!
FRRP!
...THEN I'LL JUST ENJOY THE POND WITHOUT IT!
GOODNESS, MONKEY. YOU DON'T LOOK VERY WELL.
GUP!
YO, MONKEY! I TAPED UP THE LILO, MAYBE WE CAN BOTH USE IT!
GURRR GURRRP!
SPLOOSH!
A WAVE MACHINE! BRILLIANT IDEA, MONKEY!!
BEING A METAL MONKEY SUUUUCKS!!

"JUST ONE WISH"
UPGRADE YOURSELF WITH THE MODULE!
STATS
WORKS IN ANY SIMULATION!
IT CAN MAKE YOU POWERFUL!
IT CAN MAKE YOU BRAVE!
IT CAN MAKE YOU SUPER COOL!
IT MADE ME DO METAL POOS!
IT'LL TURN YOU INTO THE YOU YOU'VE ALWAYS DREAMT OF BEING!!

BUT... I'M HAPPY AS I AM.

ARE YOU SURE, LUCKY? ONLY YOU DO ALWAYS SEEM TO BE RATHER... UNLUCKY.
OH, DO YOU THINK?

OH YEAH! IT CAN ALSO TURN YOU INTO A COW!!
MOOF!
CRUMP!
ARG!
WELL, MAYBE THERE IS ONE THING I'D LIKE TO CHANGE ABOUT MYSELF.
YES??
I'VE ALWAYS WANTED...
YESSSSSSS?
...A NICE HAT.
HAT STATS
SWIPE!
FRRP!
OH YES. THAT'S LOVELY.

LUCKY, DON'T YOU WISH FOR SOMETHING MORE?
A BIGGER HAT?
OH, WELL.
THAT'S QUITE NICE, I SUPPOSE
FRRP!
I WENT TOO BIG!
I WENT TOO BIG!!
FRRP!
OOH! A TOP HAT! NOW THAT IS NICE.
FRRP!
AT LEAST MAKE THE HAT FIRE LASERS!
NO!!
I JUST WANT A NICE HAT.
FRRP!
THAT'S ENOUGH FOR ME.
FRRP!
WHY ISN'T THAT ENOUGH FOR YOU?
FRRP!
WHAT'S MOST IMPORTANT IS THAT LUCKY IS HAPPY.
I'M NOT HAPPY. NOT ANY MORE.
FRRP!

YOU ALL WANT ME TO WEAR A DEATH HAT, SOMETHING OVER THE TOP AND DANGEROUS!
FRRP!
FRRP!
RRP!
SOMETHING TO CAUSE UNTOLD CHAOS AND DESTRUCTION!
FRP!
HOW'S THIS? IS THIS HAT GOOD ENOUGH?
ACTUALLY, THAT'S PRETTY...
SILENCE, MORTAL!!
BZZAP!
NEEYOW!
OH NO.
I LIKE THE HAT.
IT SUITS ME.
THIS IS THEIR FAULT.
IT'S THEIR FAULT.
WHATEVER HAPPENS NOW.
IT'S THEIR FAULT.

"TRANSFORM!"
AH!
WEENIE!!
DO YOU HAVE ENOUGH PIZZA TO SHARE WITH AN INTERNATIONAL SUPERSPY?
ZIIIIIIP!
OF COURSE! FOUR-CHEESE AND PICKLE, JUST HOW YOU LIKE IT!
YOU KNOW, PIG, I THOUGHT WHEN I BECAME BRAVER IT WOULD MEAN I COULD PROTECT YOU. BUT I'M NOT SURE YOU NEED IT.
CHOMP CHOMP!
I'M A PIG OF DANGER NOW, WEENIE! I ZIP IN AND OUT OF TROUBLE BEFORE ANYONE EVEN NOTICES ME!

SO MAYBE WE CAN JUST... LOOK OUT FOR EACH OTHER?
THAT WOULD BE NICE.
HEE HEE!
DID... DID THE OVEN JUST GIGGLE?
OH, CRUMBS!
IT MUST BE ONE OF SKUNKY'S INVENTIONS!
CLANG!
OR A TRAP FROM MONKEY!
CLANG!
WHATEVER IT IS, IMMA SQUEEZE THE LIFE OUT OF IT!!
SQUEEEEEEEEEEEZE!
NO! NOOOO!

IT'S ME! IT'S METAL EVE!
WELL, THAT'S UNUSUAL.
BZZP!
I USED THE MODULE TO UPGRADE MYSELF...
...SO I COULD TRANSFORM INTO ANY MACHINE!
I THOUGHT IF I COULD HIDE IN YOUR HOMES, DISGUISED AS ORDINARY APPLIANCES, THEN I COULD SECRETLY OBSERVE YOU.
I COULD UNDERSTAND YOU.
EVE, THAT'S CREEPY!
IS IT?
OH. I'LL MAKE A NOTE.
WHERE ELSE HAVE YOU HIDDEN, THEN?
WELL, I WAS A KETTLE FOR BUNNY.
HEE HEE!
I WAS A PNEUMATIC DRILL FOR AI.
B-R-R-R-R-R
H-H-HEE H-H-HEE!
I WAS A JAPANESE TOILET FOR LE FOX.
FLUSH!
BOO HOO HOO!
(I REGRET THAT NOW.)

OH! AND I WAS A METAL MONKEY FOR METAL MONKEY.
I LOOK HANDSOME!
HE THOUGHT I WAS A MIRROR.
SO WHAT HAVE YOU LEARNED FROM ALL THIS?
THAT IT WAS A TERRIBLE IDEA AND I SHOULD STOP DOING IT.
HEY, LOSERS!
AUGH
I SMELL PIZZA UP THERE! GIMME SOME!
I SHOULD GO HOME.
AM I SURE?
PRETTY SURE.
I SHOULD LISTEN TO ME. I'M VERY SMART.
WELL, OKAY, MAYBE IT'S USEFUL FOR A BIT LONGER.

"THE ARCHITECT"
SK...
SKUNKY?
YOU'VE BEEN QUIET FOR A FEW WEEKS.
WE WERE JUST WONDERING IF YOU'RE OKAY?
THE ALL-SEEING EYE!!
WHAT...WHAT HAPPENED DOWN HERE?
I TORE APART MY MACHINES FOR THE PIECES I WOULD NEED.
SKUNKY?

I'M NOT SKUNKY ANY MORE, I AM NOW KNOWN AS THE ARCHITECT!
FOR WHILE YOU WERE ALL PLAYING WITH THE MODULE, I WAS PLUGGING MYSELF DIRECTLY INTO THE SIMULATION!!
NOW I CAN NOT ONLY SEE WHAT'S HAPPENING...
...I CAN CONTROL IT, TOO!
EVERYONE GET OUT OF MY WAY! I'M METAL MONKEY, KING OF...
PANCAKES

DID YOU... DID YOU CAUSE THAT?
I THOUGHT ABOUT IT...
...AND THEN IT HAPPENED.
I AM PLUGGED INTO THE FABRIC OF OUR SUPPOSED REALITY. WHAT THE ARCHITECT DECIDES, HAPPENS.
BOOM! WE'RE ON TOP OF THE NEWLY FORMED PANCAKE MOUNTAIN!
GAH!
SKUNKY, THIS IS TOO MUCH POWER, EVEN FOR YOU!!
BOOM! WE'RE IN SPACE!!
ACK!
CAN'T
BREATHE!
OH, YEAH. SORRY. BOOM! BACK IN THE WOODS!
GAAAAASP!
YOU SEE, YOU MIGHT HAVE MAGICAL WOODLAND POWERS, BUNNY, BUT NOTHING HAPPENS HERE WITHOUT MY PERMISSION.
W... WHY?
BECAUSE A FEW MONTHS AGO YOU WERE ALL TOLD THAT YOUR WHOLE EXISTENCE HAS BEEN A LIE.
AND WHAT DID YOU DO?

YOU GOT DISTRACTED.
BUT I DIDN'T.
I'VE BEEN WATCHING.
AND I'VE SEEN WHAT YOU'VE ALL MISSED.
THE GLITCHES ARE RETURNING.
WITH MY EXTRAORDINARY POWER, I CAN COVER THEM, FOLD THEM INTO THE BACKGROUND. STOP THEM FROM DOING TOO MUCH DAMAGE.
BUT THERE ARE TOO MANY.
THE SIMULATION IS COLLAPSING, BUNNY.
WHEN IT'S GONE, WE ALL GO WITH IT!!
SO WE MIGHT AS WELL ENJOY OURSELVES.
PANCAKE?
YAY! PANCAKE!

"THAT ESCALATED QUICKLY"
STAND AGHAST! FOR THE TREMBLING CREATURE YOU ONCE KNEW AS LUCKY IS GONE. NOW THERE IS ONLY...
LUCKY THE BRUTAL!
SURVEYING HER NIGHTMARISH KINGDOM FROM UPON A THRONE MADE OF HER ENEMIES' ASHES!!

SHE'S TOO FAR AWAY.
I CAN'T HEAR HER.

SPEAK UP!
ARE YOU SAYING SOMETHING ABOUT BAKED BEANS?
YOU WILL PAY FOR THIS INSOLENCE!!
BZBBBBBB
FRRP!
CLANG!
AW. I POOPED MYSELF.
NOW LOOK HERE, LUCKY. NORMALLY I'D BE WELL UP FOR YOU LASERING MONKEY, BUT ALL THE POWER IN THAT HAT IS GOING TO YOUR HEAD.
BZBBB
THIS IS NO MERE HAT, IT IS A CROWN AND IT GRANTS ME THE STRENGTH I'VE ALWAYS YEARNED FOR!!
HEH HEH! LUCKY'S PRETTY COOL.
WHAT ARE YOU TALKING ABOUT? SHE JUST ZAPPED US!
EXACTLY!
I WANNA WORK FOR SOMEONE LIKE THAT!

HEY, LUCKY! I HAVE A BUSINESS PROPOSITION FOR YOU!!
AFTER ALL, NOW YOU'RE POWERFUL ENOUGH TO TAKE OVER THE WORLD...
...YOU'RE GOING TO NEED MY HELP.
BZBBB BBBBB
MAYBE I COULD MAKE THE TEA?
BZBBB BBBBB
I CAN HEAR MY BRAIN COOKING!
OH, FOR GOODNESS' SAKE...
MONKEY, LUCKY IS THE UNLUCKIEST CREATURE IN THE UNIVERSE!!
SOMETHING IS BOUND TO GO WRONG!
WAIT, WH... WHAT'S THAT IN THE SKY?

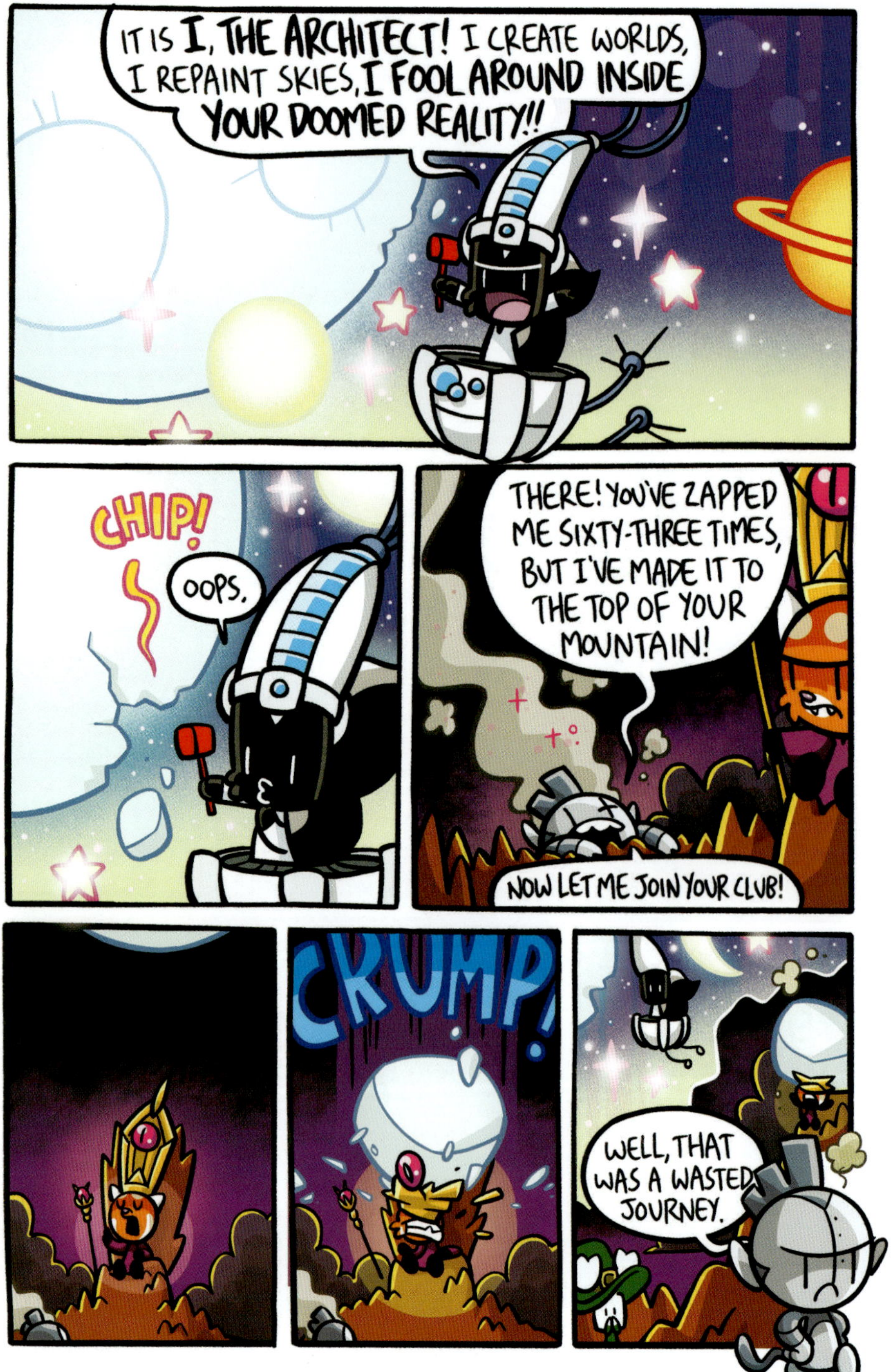
IT IS I, THE ARCHITECT! I CREATE WORLDS, I REPAINT SKIES, I FOOL AROUND INSIDE YOUR DOOMED REALITY!!
CHIP!
OOPS.
THERE! YOU'VE ZAPPED ME SIXTY-THREE TIMES, BUT I'VE MADE IT TO THE TOP OF YOUR MOUNTAIN!
NOW LET ME JOIN YOUR CLUB!
CRUMP!
WELL, THAT WAS A WASTED JOURNEY.

"THE OMNIPRESENT SKUNKY"
BUNNY, WHY HAVE YOU BROUGHT ME TO ZE TOP OF ZE TALLEST MOUNTAIN IN ZE WOODS?
I THOUGHT... I HOPED... SKUNKY MIGHT NOT BE ABLE TO FIND US UP HERE.
HANG ON.
IS THAT...
I NEVER NOTICED WE HAD TWO MOONS BEFORE.
IT'S SKUNKY! SKUNKY'S DOING THIS!

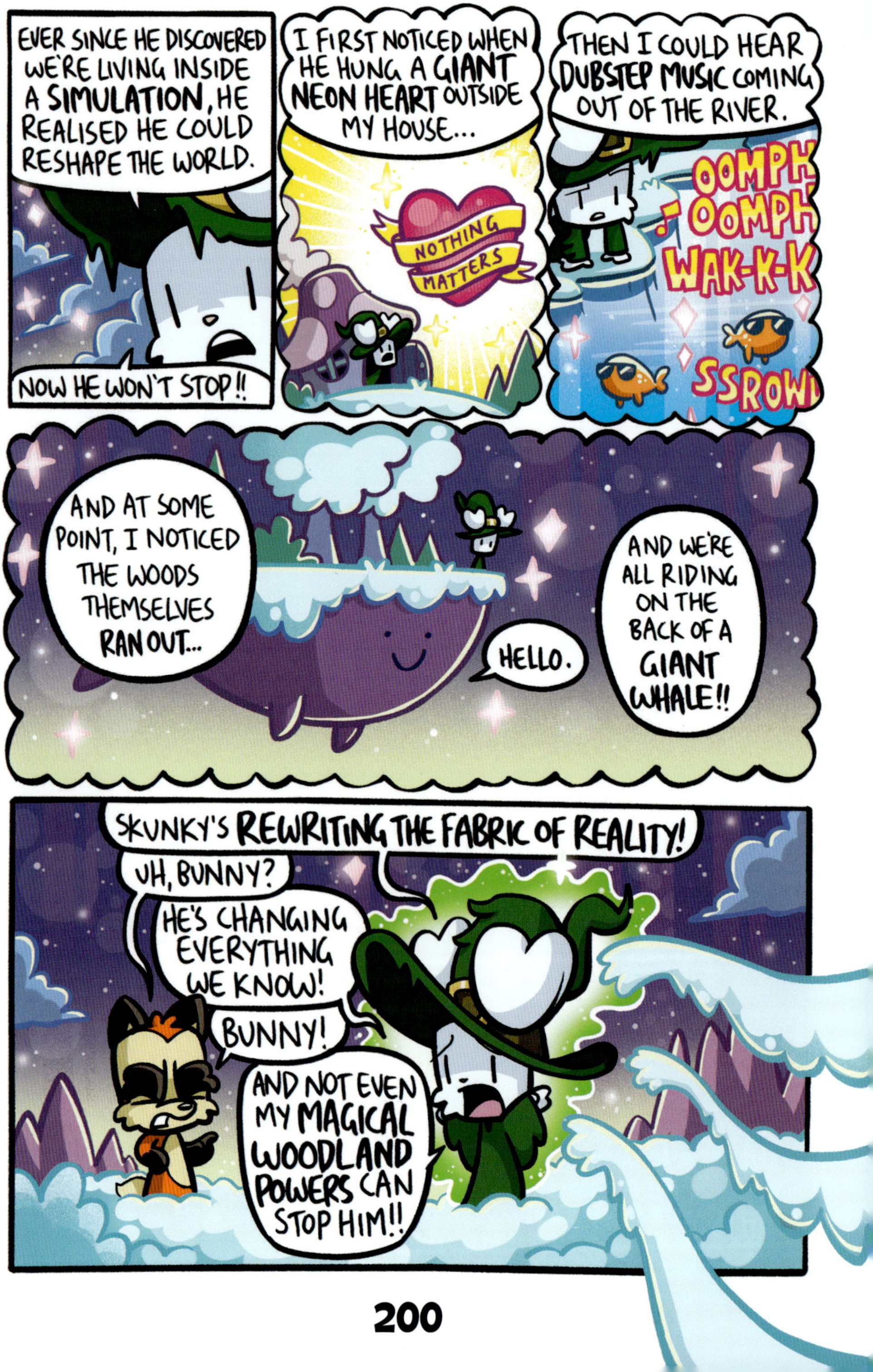
EVER SINCE HE DISCOVERED WE'RE LIVING INSIDE A SIMULATION, HE REALISED HE COULD RESHAPE THE WORLD.
NOW HE WON'T STOP!!
I FIRST NOTICED WHEN HE HUNG A GIANT NEON HEART OUTSIDE MY HOUSE...
NOTHING MATTERS
THEN I COULD HEAR DUBSTEP MUSIC COMING OUT OF THE RIVER.
OOMPH
OOMPH
WAK-K-K
AND AT SOME POINT, I NOTICED THE WOODS THEMSELVES RAN OUT...
HELLO.
AND WE'RE ALL RIDING ON THE BACK OF A GIANT WHALE!!
SKUNKY'S REWRITING THE FABRIC OF REALITY!
UH, BUNNY?
HE'S CHANGING EVERYTHING WE KNOW!
BUNNY!
AND NOT EVEN MY MAGICAL WOODLAND POWERS CAN STOP HIM!!

GMPH!!
GRAB!
I DIDN'T TAP MYSELF DIRECTLY INTO THE SIMULATION JUST TO PERFORM PARLOUR TRICKS, BUNNY.
I DID IT SO I COULD MOVE MOUNTAINS, DRAIN OCEANS, SO I COULD REARRANGE THE STARS.
AFTER ALL, THE GLITCHES ARE COMING FASTER AND FASTER...
IT WON'T BE LONG BEFORE THIS WHOLE WORLD IS GONE.

SO, I'LL JUST KEEP HIDING THEM BEHIND THINGS...
...TO KEEP US ALL EXISTING AS LONG AS POSSIBLE.
WHILE I LIVE OUT MY BEST LIFE IN THE LAST DYING GASPS OF THE UNIVERSE.
YOU ARE AN IDIOT...
HUP!!
OH COME ON, LE FOX, YOU'RE THE BIGGEST NIHILIST OF ALL OF US! SURELY YOU'LL SHARE IN MY RECKLESS ABANDON?
YOU MISTAKE MY INTENSE DISLIKE OF YOU ALL AS NOT CARING...
I CARE A LOT.
A SEETHING FURY LIKE THIS REQUIRES HUGE AMOUNTS OF ENERGY!
CHOMP!

YOU DID IT, LE FOX! YOU BIT US FREE!
I ONLY DID IT SO I COULD GO HOME.
BUT... BUT THE UNIVERSE!
KEEP ME OUT OF ZIS. YOU'RE ALL RIDICULOUS, AND YOU BELIEVE RIDICULOUS THINGS.
THAT'S IT, LE FOX!
EMBRACE YOUR OBLIVION!!
OH, DO SHUT UP.
PSST!
HEY, BUNNY.
DON'T EMBRACE YOUR OBLIVION JUST YET.

"ALL IN THIS TOGETHER"
PIZZA'S BACK ON THE MENU.. WHOA!
CURSES! MY PIGTINI!
WHEEEE!
STAY CLOSE, BUNNY!
HONKHONKKK
WHAT?
HOW DID YOU ESCAPE? WE TIED YOU UP!!
WITH RESPECT, BUNNY, A BUNCH OF CUTE ANIMALS TIED ME UP.
IT WASN'T TOO HARD TO GET FREE.

THEN I BORROWED SKUNKY'S IDEA OF AN E.M.P. HELMET, AND CONVERTED ALICE INTO MY OWN VERSION.
SIGH.
HELLO.
WITH A FEW TWEAKS, SHE'S NOW SHIELDING US FROM SKUNKY'S VIEW.
DINSSSDAAALE!
SPLOOSH
I... I THINK IT'S WORKING.
BUT WHY DID YOU COME HERE, WARDEN?
IF MY MAGICAL WOODLAND POWERS CAN'T STOP SKUNKY, I DON'T KNOW WHAT CAN.
I CAME BACK BECAUSE I FIGURED IT OUT.
I FIGURED IT ALL OUT.
I KNOW WHAT'S GOING ON!

SEE, I THOUGHT I'D CREATED THE WORLD OF BUNNY VS MONKEY AS A SIMULATION. I THOUGHT IT WAS FICTIONAL...
... BUT THEN HOW COULD YOU AND I EXIST TOGETHER? HOW COULD YOU COME INTO MY WORLD?
BECAUSE...
BECAUSE I'M IN A SIMULATION TOO!!
ACTION COW RAN OUT OF FARTS!
PARP!
OH. NO. THERE'S ONE.
CRUMP!
PRRP! PRRP!
I CREATED YOU, BUNNY, I CREATED ALL OF YOU... BUT WHO CREATED ME?
WAIT, SO... WE'RE A SIMULATION... INSIDE A BIGGER SIMULATION?
YES! THAT'S IT!
SOMETHING ELSE IS BEHIND ALL OF THIS!

AND WHATEVER, OR WHOEVER, IT IS, THEY MADE A MISTAKE.
THE GLITCHES!
THE WHOLE SIMULATION IS BROKEN!
I THOUGHT THE GLITCHES WOULD TEAR EVERYTHING APART... BUT NOW SKUNKY'S ON A POWER TRIP, HE'LL PROBABLY DO IT FIRST.
MY NAME ... IS THE ARCHITECT.
AUGH!
AND YOUR HAT FELL OFF.
QUICKLY, BUNNY! THERE ISN'T MUCH TIME!
TO DO WHAT?
TO FIX THIS!
SOMEWHERE, BEYOND OUR UNDERSTANDING, SOME KIND OF SUPERCOMPUTER IS RUNNING ALL OF THIS!!
WHOA!
BUT IT WILL HAVE LEFT A BACK DOOR, A DIRECT LINK OUT OF HERE...
LOOK FOR SOMETHING OUT OF PLACE.
SOMETHING UNUSUALLY INTELLIGENT!!
THIS IS FINE.
TOTALLY FINE.
FOUND IT.

(WITH APOLOGIES TO KC GREEN)

"FINALLY HAPPY"
SO, LET ME GET THIS STRAIGHT.
THE WARDEN CREATED US IN A SIMULATION...
...BUT IT TURNS OUT HE WAS ALREADY IN A SIMULATION...
...CREATED BY SOME KIND OF SUPERCOMPUTER...
...AND WE THINK THAT SUPERCOMPUTER MIGHT BE...
...METAL EVE!!
I AM TECHNICALLY A SUPER-COMPUTER.
SO IT'S QUITE POSSIBLE!
AND IF EVE'S MANUAL IS CORRECT, I SHOULD BE ABLE TO SWITCH OFF THE SIMULATION BY PRESSING THIS BUTTON.
BOOP!
HONK HONK GOES THE HORSE!
WEE WEE GOES THE FART!
I FARTED IN MY SHOES, MUMMY!
NOPE, WRONG BUTTON.
RRGH! WHY IS YOUR MANUAL SO CONFUSING?

LET ME HAVE A LOOK.
YOU? MONKEY, HOW CAN YOU HELP?
SNIFF!
ROBOTS UNDERSTAND ROBOTS.
HANG ON, IF YOU SWITCH OFF THE SIMULATION, WON'T WE ALL STOP EXISTING?
WELL, YES.
BUT I... I LIKE EXISTING.
ME TOO.
WHY ON EARTH WOULD WE WANT TO STOP?
BECAUSE THIS ISN'T REALITY. IT'S A LIE. IT'S ALL A LIE. THE REAL WORLD EXISTS OUTSIDE OF EVE'S SIMULATION.
BOOP!
FART FART FART!
SHOES SHOES SHOES!
NOPE, STILL NOT RIGHT.
WELL, WHATEVER VERSION OF ME EXISTS IN THE REAL WORLD, IT CAN'T BE AS COOL AS THIS ONE.
FOR THE FIRST TIME EVER, I'M COMFORTABLE WITH WHO I AM!
ME TOO.
ME TOO.
MOO MOO.
I'M FINE EITHER WAY, TO BE HONEST.

I... I HAVE TO AGREE! I HAVE LEARNT SO MUCH INSIDE THIS SIMULATION. I AM FINALLY STARTING TO UNDERSTAND WHAT IT MEANS TO BE ALIVE!
I'M SORRY IF THIS IS MY FAULT, BUT I DON'T WANT IT TO END!
EVE! COME BACK!
WE MUST STAY HERE, IN THIS NON-REALITY WHERE WE'RE HAPPY!
WOO!
CLANG!
OH, HANG ON.
SKUNKY ALREADY BROKE IT ALL, DIDN'T HE.
AHA!
THE GLITCHES BROKE THIS WORLD. I'M JUST PLAYING WITH THE PIECES!
WHAT DO I DO? WHAT DO I DOOOO?
BOOP!
THERE! BUTTON B6 FOR A FACTORY RESET.
TOLD YOU I COULD DO IT.
GASP!
OH, THANK GOODNESS...
IT... IT WAS ALL JUST A SIMULATION.
PLAYING INSIDE MY BRAIN!

BUT IT FELT SO REAL.
SO VIVID.
AS IF WE HAD ALL BEEN IN THERE FOR MONTHS.
FOR YEARS.
SO LONG, IN FACT, I'VE FORGOTTEN WHAT THE REAL WORLD LOOKS LIKE.
HUH. WERE THE FLOWERS ALWAYS THIS BIG?
CHOMP!
!!!
SHRIEK! I WASN'T RUNNING THINGS AT ALL.
THIS IS METALSTEVE'S SIMULATION...
...AND WE'RE STILL STUCK INSIDE IT!!

"METAL STEVE'S WORLD"
STUCK IN A MINIATURE WORLD WITH A MINIATURE MECHANICAL MONSTER!
DESTROY!!
BZZAPP!
IT WASN'T ME! I'M NOT THE SUPERCOMPUTER! METAL STEVE MUST HAVE BEEN RUNNING THIS SIMULATION ALL ALONG!!

BZZAP!
BZZAP!

METAL STEVE'S BEHIND ALL THIS?
I GUESS SO!!

ALL THIS TIME, WE'VE BEEN STUCK IN A FANTASY WORLD OF HIS MAKING!
WELL, THAT DOESN'T SEEM RIGHT.
I JUST CAN'T PICTURE IT. THAT BIG OLD TRASH CAN RUNNING A HYPER-REALISTIC SIMULATION OF THE ENTIRE UNIVERSE?
NOW YOU MENTION IT, IT DOES SEEM A BIT ...FAR-FETCHED.
WELL, I DON'T SEE ANY OTHER SUPERCOMPUTERS AROUND HERE!
WHAT?

OH! YES! IT WAS ME!
I AM THE DESIGNER OF ALL YOUR DESTINIES!
TOBY'S LITTLE 'BUNNY VS MONKEY' GAME WAS CUTE, BUT I ALWAYS KNEW HE COULD ACHIEVE EVEN GREATER THINGS!!
SO, I CREATED THIS SIMULATION AND PUT YOU, AND YOURS, INSIDE IT, SO I COULD ENSURE A SUCCESSFUL OUTCOME.
ALICE...
BUT WHY?
BECAUSE...
BECAUSE I JUST WANT YOU TO LOVE ME, TOBY!
BWOOM!
OKAY I LIED.
IT WASN'T ME.
BZZZ
IT WASN'T ME!
BZZT! BAD DREAM!
BAD DREAM!

OH, THANK GOODNESS!
THEY WERE GETTING A BIT ANNOYING.
FRRP!
BUT WAIT... NOW WHO'S SIMULATION IS THIS?
LE SIGH.
YOU'RE USING ZE WRONG WORD.
LE FOX! IS THIS YOUR SIMULATION?
ZEY'RE NOT SIMULATIONS.
ZEY ARE DREAMS!
WITHIN DREAMS!
WITHIN DREAMS!
AFTER ALL, WHAT GREATER SUPERCOMPUTER IS ZERE THAN ZE BRAIN?
YOU WON'T GET INSIDE MY BRAIN. I'M WEARING METAL PANTS!!
OKAY, I'M GOING TO NEED YOU ALL TO WAKE UP NOW.

"THE ENDLESS"
HONK HONK
FARPITY FARP
BLIP BLOP
AWOOGA
BAP!
PLOP PLOP
WEE WOO
BIP BIP BIP
BAROOO!
NOW VERSE TWO!

ACTION BEAVER, WAKE UP!!
GARUMP!
SNCKK!!
AWOOGA
AWOOGA

WE DID IT! WE'RE OUT OF ACTION BEAVER'S DREAM!
BUT WHOSE DREAM IS THIS?
AWOOGA AWOOGA
UH OH.
A MISSILE SILO HIDDEN INSIDE A VOLCANO? SAVE YOURSELVES, THIS IS A JOB FOR CODENAME P.I.G.!!
PYEW! PYEW! PYEW! PYEW! PYEW! PYEW!
PIG, NO!!
WAKE UP!!
CLONK!
AWW.
OOH! A CLASS FIVE STAINLESS-STEEL FRYING PAN!
OH NO. THIS IS MY DREAM!

BLAT!
AWW.
I'M NORMAL ME AGAIN.
LOL! NOT ME, SUCKER!
I DON'T CARE IF THIS IS A DREAM, I'M GOING TO BE LUCKY THE BRUTAL FOR AS LONG AS POSSIBLE!
HAVE SOME OF THAT!
BZZZZP!
ARGH!
I DID IT! I FINALLY WORKED OUT WHAT I WANT TO BE!

I AM AI, THE CLOAKED NINJA!! SNEAKING AROUND IN THE LAND OF SHADOWS, LIGHTING MY PATH WITH ELECTRICAL POWERS!
FZZAP!
ENOUGH WITH THESE RIDICULOUS DREAMS!
FOR YOU ONLY EVER EXISTED IN THE MIND OF THE MANIACAL BADGER!!
AND NOW, I'M CHOOSING TO FORGET YOU ALL.
AHEM.
WHAT?
OH.
REALLY?
AGAIN?
PHEW! WHAT A NIGHTMARE!
I REALLY NEED TO STOP DREAMING ABOUT THAT INFERNAL BADGER!
GUH!
WHAT A NIGHTMARE!
I REALLY NEED TO STOP EATING GOAT'S CHEESE BEFORE BED.

WELL, WHY DID YOU DREAM YOURSELF INTO MY HOUSE?
AH, WHO AM I TO COMPLAIN? IN YOUR DREAM, THE WOODS ARE BACK TO NORMAL...
...WHICH MAKES ME POWERFUL!!
SO HOW ABOUT WE FINISH THIS ONCE AND FOR ALL!
NICE TRY BUNNY, BUT THIS IS MY DREAM...
STRE-E-ETCH
...AND YOU CAN'T DRAW ANY POWER FROM THE WOODLANDS...
...IF I TURN IT ALL INTO METAL!
CLUNK!
GASP!

CLUNK!
CLUNK
NYAH HA HAAAA!!
THAT'S IT!
RUN, BUNNY!
YOUR MAGICAL POWERS ARE USELESS!!
UNK!
TRIP!
OH, FOR GOODNESS' SAKE.

LE FOX! I DON'T REMEMBER DREAMING ABOUT YOU!
ZAT'S BECAUSE THIS IS NOT YOUR DREAM, MONKEY.
... IT IS BUNNY'S.
HUH?
NOOOO! DON'T WAKE UP, BUNNY! DON'T WAKE UP!!
GNYAH!
WHAT... WHAT A WEIRD DREAM.

EVERYTHING WAS A SIMULATION, INSIDE ANOTHER SIMULATION, INSIDE A DREAM INSIDE A DREAM INSIDE WHO KNOWS HOW MANY OTHER DREAMS!
BUT AT LEAST I'M AWAKE NOW.
BACK IN THE...
REAL...
WORLD!
THE GLITCHES!
THEY'RE HERE TOO!
BUT... BUT HOW?!

BECAUSE YOU'RE STILL **ASLEEP**, BUNNY...
SHRIEK!
... YOU'RE STILL INSIDE THE DREAM.
SHRIEK!
...AND YOU'RE THE ONLY ONE WHO CAN WAKE YOURSELF UP!!
SHRIIIIIIIIIIIIIEK!!

"THE RELEASE"
THIS IS MY DREAM.
IN HERE I'M ALL POWERFUL.
IN HERE THE GLITCHES CAN'T HURT ME.

SKUNKY! WHATEVER'S GOING ON, YOU'RE IN MY WORLD NOW!
REMEMBER WHAT THE GLITCHES ARE, BUNNY.
THEY'RE ERRORS.
IN HERE I HOLD ALL THE POWER!
WAIT.
WHAT JUST CHANGED?

GOOOSH
THE GLITCHES STARTED WHEN THE SOFTWARE COULDN'T FUNCTION.
NYAH!
WHAT... WHAT'S THE SOFTWARE?
THIS IS YOUR DREAM, BUNNY.
MAYBE THERE'S SOMETHING YOUR BRAIN HASN'T WORKED OUT YET.
GLOOP!
WAIT.
ARE THE GLITCHES INSIDE MY BRAIN?
MAYBE THERE'S SOMETHING IT CAN'T.
BUT I FEEL GREAT! I'M ALL I EVER WANTED TO BE. BUNNY, PROTECTOR OF THE WOODS!!
BAM
BUT... BUT EVEN I CAN'T STOP THE GLITCHES!

FWPP!
WHERE...
WHERE AM I?
YOUR MIND SHOWED US WHAT WE COULD BE.
NYAH!

IT CREATED A WHOLE ELABORATE STORYLINE TO LET US REACH OUR FULL POTENTIAL.
NYAH!
BUT IT WON'T...
...LET...
YOU.
NYAH!
HONK?
NYAH!
DON'T LOOK AT ME, I'M NOT INVOLVED IN ANY OF THIS.
NYAH!
YOUR OWN MIND COULDN'T PROCESS THE IDEA THAT YOU COULD EVER BE POWERFUL...
...AND IT IMMEDIATELY STARTED SHUTTING YOU DOWN
NYAH! NYAH!
BAM BAM!
BAM BAM! BAM!
BUT I AM POWERFUL.
I'M THE PROTECTOR OF THE WOODS!

THAT'S TOO MUCH RESPONSIBILITY FOR THE BUNNY YOU KNOW TO HANDLE.
SO I'M...
...SCARED?
YOU DON'T HAVE TO BE
ALL THIS...BECAUSE I DON'T FEEL WORTHY...
...BUT I AM WORTHY...
...I DESERVE TO BE STRONG.

THAT'S IT, BUNNY!
BAM!
I DON'T NEED TO BE AFRAID ANY MORE.
BECAUSE I'M BUNNY...
BAM!
...PROTECTOR OF THESE WOODS...
BAM!
...AND I BELIEVE IN MYSELF!!
BAM! BAM! BAM! BAM! BAM! BAM! BAM! BAM! BAM! BAM! BAM! BAM! BAM!
BUNNY! WAKE UP!!
AND NOW HE'S CHASING US WITH THE TURKEY!!
GOBBLE GOBBLE, LOSERS!
F-WOOM!
WHILE YOU WERE HAVING A BOXING DAY LIE-IN, MONKEY BURNT THE POTATOES!!
THE FESTIVE SEASON HAS BEGUN!!

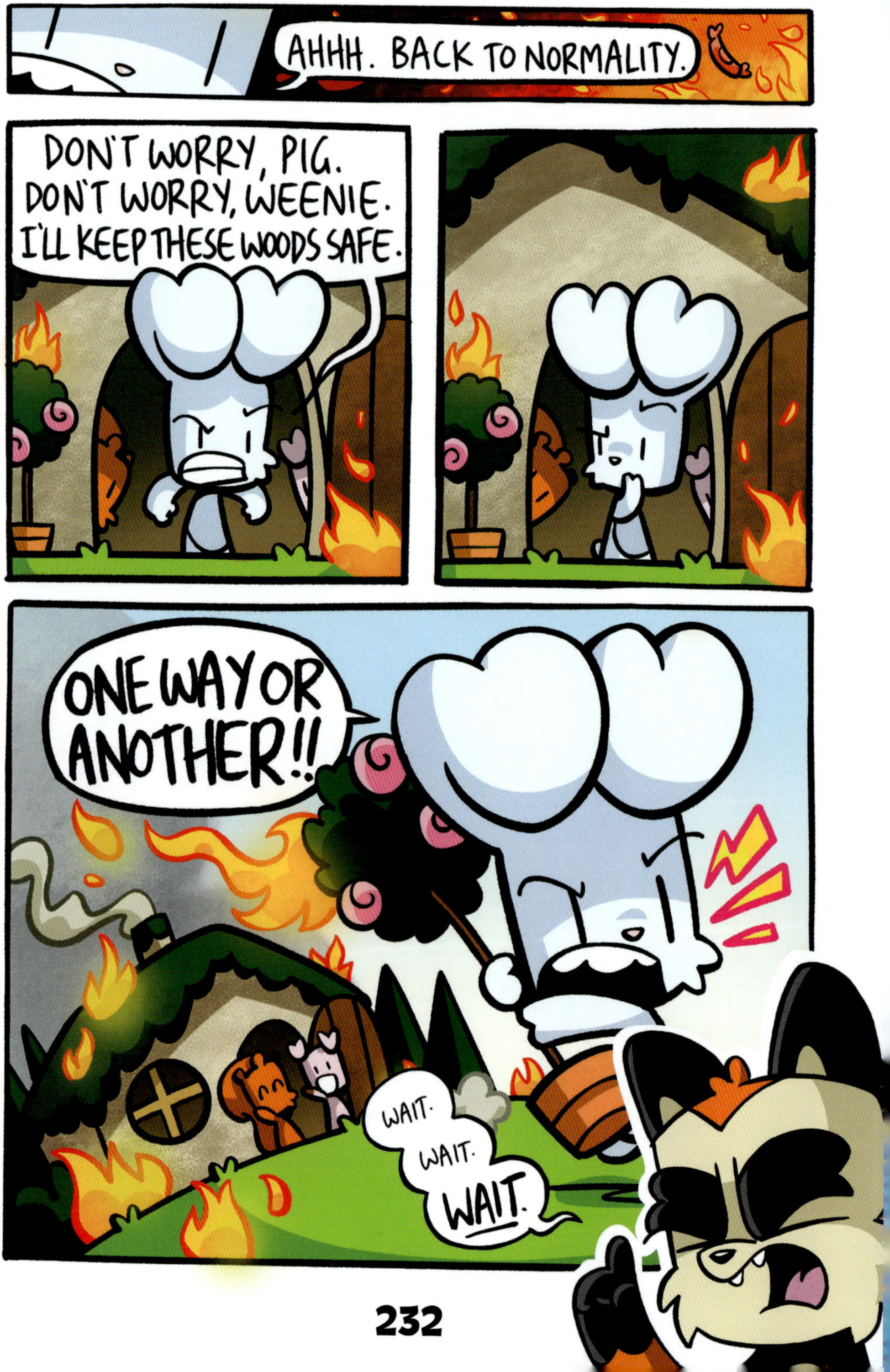
AHHH. BACK TO NORMALITY.
DON'T WORRY, PIG. DON'T WORRY, WEENIE. I'LL KEEP THESE WOODS SAFE.
ONE WAY OR ANOTHER!!
WAIT.
WAIT.
WAIT.

-AN-

EPILOGUE

IN WHICH LE FOX TRIES TO COMPREHEND WHERE ALL THIS HAS LEFT US.

SO ARE YOU A MAGIC BUNNY NOW?
NO.
LE SIGH.
AGAIN.
SO EVERYTHING THAT HAS HAPPENED, ALL OF ZE GLITCHING, IT WAS ALL JUST A DREAM?
WELL... SORT OF.
LE SIGH SIGH.

YOU SEE, WHEN I RETURNED FROM THE MOLECULAR STREAM, I RETAINED SOME OF ITS POWER...
FZZP!
I WENT TO SLEEP THAT NIGHT FEELING VERY EXCITED...
..AND I DREAMT OF ALL THE THINGS I MIGHT BE ABLE TO DO AS A SUPER POWERFUL BUNNY...

BUT EVERY TIME I IMAGINED MYSELF USING THESE POWERS...
PLINK!
PLUNK!
PLUNK!
...MY MIND SHUT THE DREAM DOWN...
PLOMP!
PLOMP!
PLOMP!
...AND STARTED AGAIN.

THE GLITCHING, THE SIMULATIONS, THE MODULE, IT WAS ALL JUST MY BRAIN TRYING TO MAKE SENSE OF WHAT IT WAS FEELING...
ME?
POWERFUL?
IT COULDN'T CONCEIVE OF SUCH A THING.

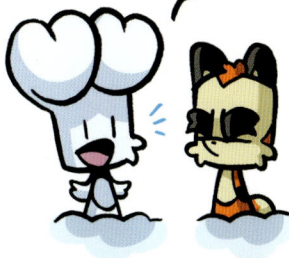

AS IT HAPPENS, MY POWERS HAVE FADED ANYWAY. I MUST BE TOO FAR FROM THE MOLECULAR STREAM.
BUT I DON'T NEED THEM.
YOU JUST NEEDED TO FIND CONFIDENCE IN YOURSELF.
EXACTLY.
WHUMP!

THEY TRUSSED UP MY TURKEYTRON!!
AND BESIDES, I'LL ALWAYS BE OKAY AS LONG AS I HAVE FRIENDS.
ALTHOUGH, IT WAS KINDA COOL BEING SUPER STACKED!!
I WAS AN AWESOME SECRET AGENT!!
MY HELMET WAS ACE!
I DON'T MISS BEING A TOILET.
WAIT, WHAT?
CLOAKED NINJA POWERRRRS!!

HUFF HUFF!
BZZZP!
HRRGHH!
GOBBLE?

HOW -TO- DRAW...
WIZARD BUNNY!
WHEN DRAWING ANY CHARACTER, IT OFTEN HELPS TO START WITH THEIR HEAD...
A LOT OF CHARACTERS HAVE A KEY LINE, GET THAT RIGHT, AND ALL THE OTHER SHAPES TEND TO WORK AROUND IT...
OUR KEY LINE FOR WIZARD BUNNY IS THE BRIM OF HIS HAT!
USE THE KEY LINE TO BUILD THE REST OF THE HAT... ADD DETAILS ONCE YOU'VE FOUND ITS BASIC SHAPE!
DON'T FORGET TO ADD BUNNY'S EARS.
FOR BUNNY'S BODY, DRAW A LUMP UNDER HIS HEAD..
ADD BASIC SHAPES FOR HIS ARMS AND LEGS...
SAUSAGES FOR ARMS!
CIRCLES FOR FEET!
THEN ADD SOME DETAILS - FINGERS, LEAVES, SLEEVES!
AAAND WE'RE DONE!

PEW! PEW PEW!
FZZZCK!
SPLOSH SPLOSH SPLOOOOOSH!
WAIT, NO, WHAT?
WHAT?
WHAT?
RRRGH!
I'M MORE CONFUSED THAN EVER!!

HOW TO DRAW
BUFF WEENIE!
LIKE WITH BUNNY, LET'S START WITH THE HEAD FIRST...
1
2
3
BUFF WEENIE'S KEYLINE IS HER SHOULDERS. THIS LINE CAN STRETCH + MOVE AS SHE DOES...
ARCH THE LINE DEPENDING ON HOW WEENIE IS STANDING.
ONCE WE HAVE THE SHOULDERS, WE CAN DRAW HUGE SAUSAGE SHAPES COMING OFF IT FOR WEENIE'S ARMS!
ADD A FIST!
AND ANOTHER ARM...
CHEAT THE FIST!
CURLED SAUSAGE!
NOW FINISH OFF THE UPPER BODY LIKE SO...
ADD A WAIST!
TWO LEGS!
DON'T FORGET WEENIE'S TAIL!
AAAND WE'RE DONE!

HOW -TO- DRAW
ACTION COW!
FOR COW ACTION BEAVER WE'RE GOING TO START A LITTLE DIFFERENTLY. THIS SHAPE FORMS THE WHOLE BODY...
ADD A FEW DETAILS!
LEGS AND UDDERS!
DON'T FORGET A PATTERN, AND A TAIL!
NOW WE CAN ADD A HEAD TO THE FRONT OF THE BODY USING THIS SHAPE...
WE DRAW ACTION BEAVER'S HELMET ON TOP OF IT...
ADD IN A FEW DETAILS...
TARGET!
NOSTRILS!
BELL!
AAAND WE'RE DONE! FART AWAY, ACTION COW!
ARF!
PARP!
PRRP!

MORE HILARIOUS HIJINKS IN THE FULL SERIES OF
BUNNY VS MONKEY
JAMIE SMART'S
BUNNY VS MONKEY
RISE OF THE MANIACAL BADGER
CAN THE FUNNIEST EVER RIVALS ...WORK TOGETHER?!
JAMIE SMART'S
BUNNY VS MONKEY
BUNNY BONANZA!
PLUS MORE SOON!
COLLECT THEM ALL AT
THEPHOENIXCOMIC.SHOP
AND ALL GOOD BOOKSHOPS

ENTER THE WORLD OF
JAMIE SMART'S
FLEMBER
DISCOVER THE MAGICAL POWER OF FLEMBER, WITH BOY-INVENTOR DEV AND HIS BEST FRIEND, BOJA THE BEAR!

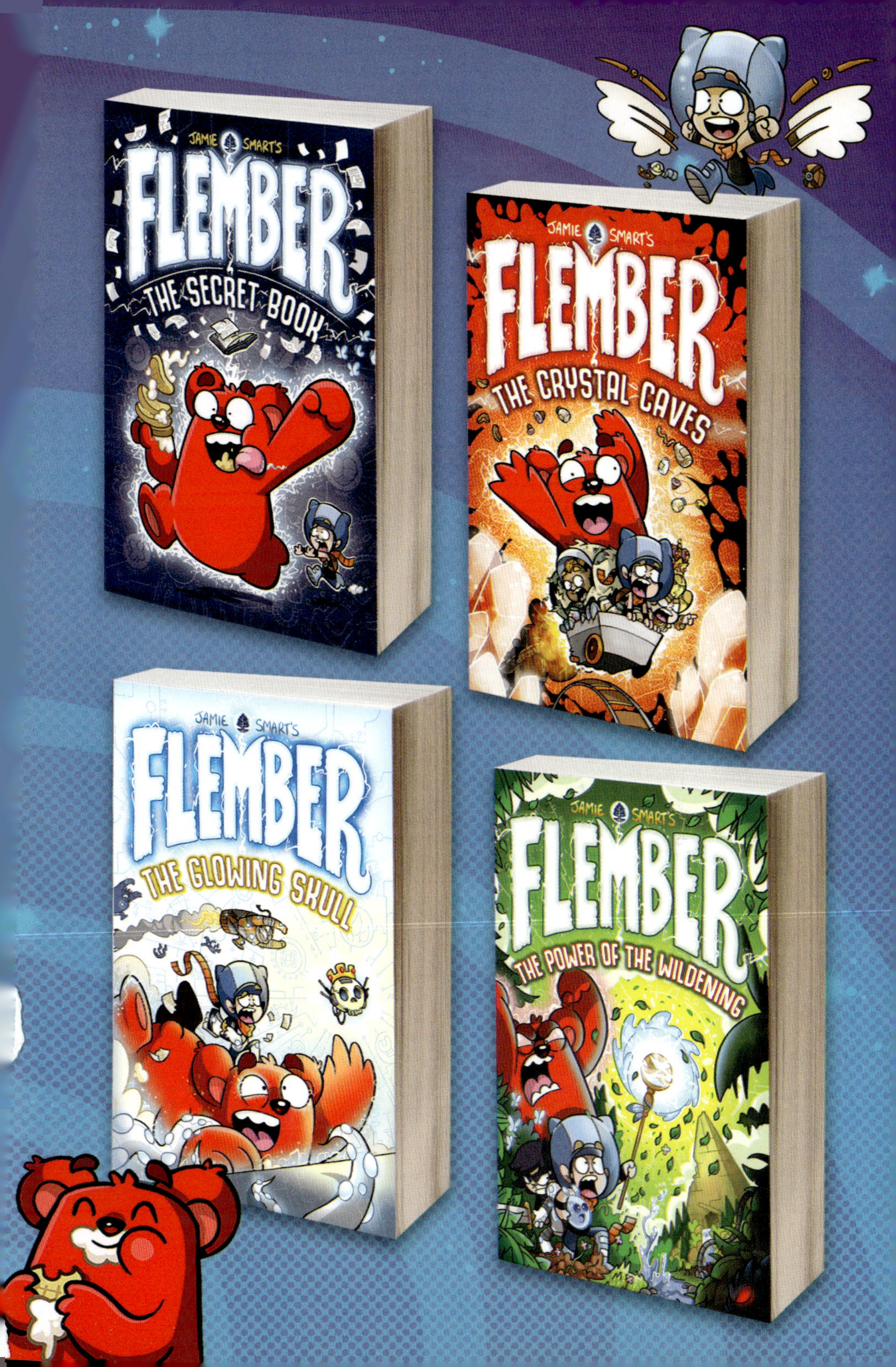
JAMIE SMART'S
FLEMBER
THE SECRET BOOK
JAMIE SMART'S
FLEMBER
THE CRYSTAL CAVES
JAMIE SMART'S
FLEMBER
THE GLOWING SKULL
JAMIE SMART'S
FLEMBER
THE POWER OF THE WILDENING

LOOSHKIN

THE MADDEST CAT IN THE WORLD!

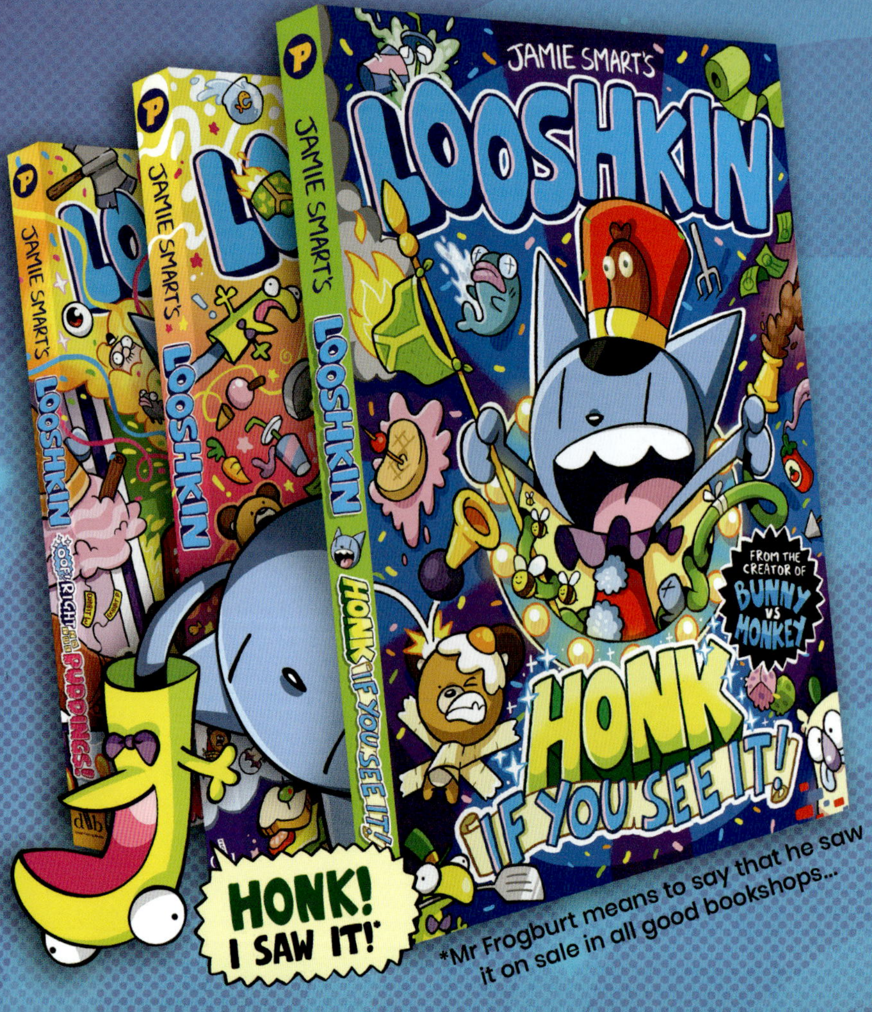

*Mr Frogburt means to say that he saw it on sale in all good bookshops...

YOU'VE NEVER MET A CAT LIKE LOOSHKIN BEFORE!
LOOSHKIN!
LOOSHKIN!
LOOSHKIN, WHAT HAVE YOU DONE?!!
THBTH TPTH BTH!
'JAMIE SMART IS A COMIC GENIUS'
PHILIP REEVE
'YOU WILL CRY WITH LAUGHTER'
STEPHEN L. HOLLAND, COMICS LAUREATE
'OUTRAGEOUSLY FUN... IN A CLASS OF ITS OWN FOR SILLINESS!'
BOOKTRUST

SPECIAL PREVIEW!

***The Phoenix* is the only place you can read the NEWEST *Megalomaniacs*!**

THE SKILLS HUB

DRAW YOUR MONSTERS

With Zak Simmonds-Hurn

WE'RE LEARNING HOW TO DRAW MONSTER PARTS, SO WE CAN BUILD OUR OWN MONSTER!
EYES, TEETH AND FANGS

MONSTROUS EYEBALLS

LET'S MAKE THOSE PEEPERS INTO CREEPERS!

JUST START WITH CIRCLES! ONE FOR THE EYEBALL, ONE FOR THE IRIS, ONE FOR THE PUPIL, LIKE THIS.

TO ADD SOME SHINE, LEAVE A SMALL WHITE CIRCLE IN THE PUPIL AND A CURVED RECTANGLE OVERLAPPING PART OF THE IRIS.

TO MAKE AN EYE-BALL LOOK VEINY, DRAW THIN, WIGGLY, BRANCHING LINES AROUND THE EDGE OF THE EYE.

YOU COULD PUT YOUR EYES ON STALKS FOR A REALLY STRANGE LOOK! JUST IMAGINE THERE'S A HOSEPIPE COMING OUT OF THE BACK OF THE EYE, CONNECTING IT TO YOUR MONSTER'S HEAD!

CREATURE FEATURES

LET'S GIVE YOUR TEETH AND EYES A HOME!

I STARTED WITH A VERY SIMPLE OUTLINE FOR THE MONSTER'S HEAD AND DREW A CIRCLE FOR THE EYE AND A BIG MOUTH SHAPE.

I DREW A PUPIL ON THE EYEBALL AND THEN ADDED SOME TEETH IN THE MOUTH. I DREW THEM NARROWER AND CLOSER AT EITHER SIDE OF THE MOUTH TO SHOW THAT THE TEETH CURVE AROUND IN A 'U' SHAPE.

LASTLY, I FILLED IN THE REST OF THE MOUTH – EVERYTHING THAT ISN'T TEETH!

TRY DIFFERENT TYPES OF EYES WITH DIFFERENT TYPES OF TEETH. THERE ARE SO MANY POSSIBILITIES, SO HAVE FUN PLAYING AROUND!

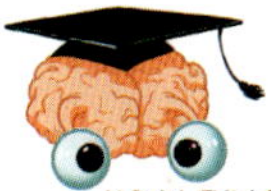

PROFESSOR BRAYN'S MONSTER TIPS!

MANY THINGS WILL AFFECT HOW YOU DESIGN YOUR MONSTER. HERE ARE SOME THINGS TO CONSIDER BEFORE YOU BEGIN.

BIG CHUNKY ROUNDED TEETH AND SIMPLE EYES MAKE YOUR MONSTER LOOK LESS THREATENING.

LOTS OF SHARP TEETH AND WEIRD EYES WILL GIVE YOUR MONSTER THE SCARE-FACTOR!

BUILDING OUR MONSTER:

We've just learnt to draw eyes and mouths! Let's add those to a monster!

Learn how to draw horns, tails and much more in *The Phoenix*!

There are more PRO DRAWING TIPS just like this, every week in *The Phoenix*!

SPECIAL PREVIEW!

Find brand-new SHORTS and hilarious comics in *The Phoenix*!

Wasn't that AWESOME?! This is just a tiny glimpse!

DRAGON GUARD
FORGED IN *STAR-FIRE* AND UNITED BY *VALOUR*, THE DRAGON GUARD MUST DEFEND THE *ELDER DRAGON EGG*, HIDDEN IN THE HEART OF OUR SUN, AGAINST THE *FORCES OF EVIL.*
ART BY ZAK SIMMONDS-HURN – STORY BY TEAM PHOENIX
SOMEWHERE ON THE EDGE OF OUR SOLAR SYSTEM...
SHHIING!
KLANG!
SHING!
KRUNCH
BOOM
KROOOM!
TAKE THAT, *TITANITE SCUM!*
MS ISABELLE, MORE OF THEM ARE ON THE WAY!